something more than this

ALSO BY BARBIE BOHRMAN

Promise Me

Playing It Safe

Starting Over

BARBIE BOHRMAN

something more than this

Montlake
Romance

Text copyright © 2016 Barbie Bohrman
All rights reserved.

Published by Montlake Romance, Seattle

www.apub.com

Amazon, the Amazon logo, and Montlake Romance are trademarks of Amazon.com, Inc., or its affiliates.

ISBN-13: 9781503935167
ISBN-10: 1503935167

Cover design by Eileen Carey

Printed in the United States of America

To anyone who finds true love and a best friend all rolled into one . . . consider yourself one of the lucky ones. And to Bryan Ferry, for writing such a beautiful song, which has stayed with me all these years later.

xo, B

PROLOGUE

At thirteen, a very close friendship blossomed into love, although unrequited.

It seems impossible to be *in love* at that age. That the mind of a thirteen-year-old could not come close to comprehending the intense, almost blinding emotions that arrest your heart and stutter your breathing until somehow, rational thought is nothing but a temporary reprieve from the constant buzzing in your head.

But for me, it was true.

And it was also true that he would go on to break my heart into a million pieces a few years later.

I can look back now and cherish the friendship we had, but the nagging question remains . . . what if?

Years later I would be faced with this same question, but this time the tables would be turned and the blurred lines of friendship would make it impossible to see what was right in front of me all along.

CHAPTER ONE

T here! *That's* what was missing. Now it's perfect.

I read over the article for what seems like the millionth time before e-mailing it to my editor with six minutes to spare. Phew! That one was close. Not that I haven't grazed a deadline before. Sometimes I've come within a minute or two, which always gets me a stern talking to or a look that's supposed to terrify me into submission by said editor. But coming from Dylan Sterling, editor in chief of the *Florida Observer* and my boss, the lectures and looks don't terrify me at all.

That's probably because Dylan couldn't scare me even if he was dressed as the grim reaper, hiding in one of the closets in my apartment waiting to jump out at me. That megawatt smile of his will always give him away. We've known each other since we met at our college newspaper. After he had skimmed through a handful of my clippings from my high school newspaper by way of an interview, he immediately said to me, "Katy, I think this is the beginning of a beautiful friendship."

And it definitely has been.

He was a senior and took this newbie freshman under his experienced wing and became my mentor. Dylan taught me all I needed to know to survive this business and then some. And when I was fresh out of college, he took a gamble on me yet again and gave me my very first job as a journalist at my hometown newspaper.

It's a midsized daily newspaper based in Fort Lauderdale that has a circulation of just over seventy thousand subscribers. I cover the local high school sports beat, focusing on high school football, which is a pretty big deal around here. Especially since one of the teams went to the state championship last season. Unfortunately, they lost. But this season I think they have a much better shot at winning the whole enchilada.

I've been at the *Observer* for the last four years, and at least once a week I'm precariously close to missing my deadline. It's not from a lack of trying. It's more that I'm a bit of a perfectionist.

Actually, I'm a *huge* perfectionist.

But that's what makes me good at my job. Actually, that's what makes me great at my job. It also helps that I love what I do with every fiber of my being.

My older brothers, Jonathan and Simon, instilled in me a lot of love, respect, and admiration for the game of football. Unfortunately, being a girl—well, now a woman—I can't play the actual game anymore without it being ridiculously painful. But instead of fighting the good fight that some girls do—and it is a damn good fight—I decided to take my love of the game and turn it into a career in sports journalism. Eventually, I hope to make it to the big time: covering the NFL for the larger newspaper in circulation in South Florida and then accomplishing my goal of working in any way, shape, or form at *Sports Illustrated*.

So here I am at twenty-five years old, doing what I love to do on a daily basis and enjoying every minute of it. The bustling of the newsroom around me never ceases to pump the blood in my veins. It reminds me why I have to work harder than most people here.

It takes thick skin to be a woman sports reporter. There are folks who assume that there is no possible way I could know what I'm writing or talking about, so I get a curious amount of hate mail every week. And I do read it . . . can't really help myself. But those letters fuel the fire to prove the naysayers wrong and show them that a woman can do this job just as well as any man could, if not better.

I'd like to think that I do.

My phone starts to vibrate then, looking like it's trying its hardest to skip across my desk and escape. I don't even have to look to see who it is before I swipe the screen and start talking.

"You're losing your touch," I say. "You usually call me within a minute after I send you my final copy. What's it been? Like, two or three minutes?"

"What can I say? I was in awe of your prose for a minute more than usual," Dylan says.

I grin at his praise. "So you liked it?"

"It's great, Katy."

"Thank you."

He draws in a breath, then says, "You're welcome. And thank *you* for making the deadline."

"Dylan—"

"Katy," he cuts in with that tone that I know means business. "Do you mind adhering to it a little more thoughtfully? I mean, I don't want to put you out or anything, but it is there for a reason."

My eyes dart around the newsroom and I feel as if everyone is staring at me as I'm being dressed down. When I'm sure they are all going about their business, I say, "I know and I will. Thanks, Dylan."

"No problem, that's what I'm here for, right?"

"Right."

"Okay, Miss Know-It-All, are you ready?" He clears his throat, then asks, "Who has the distinction of being the only player of Hispanic heritage to be drafted with the first overall pick in the NFL draft?"

I hear him rip the page off of his sports-themed desk calendar as I'm thinking of the answer. Every day he'll call or text me the question from his NFL calendar, and I usually get it right, much to his surprise. He's been quizzing me ever since I waltzed into his office one day and snatched that year's calendar off his desk and started answering question after question in quick succession. Since then, I've been buying him one as a gag gift for Christmas every year. The first year, he was convinced that I read every single question before I gave it to him. So I made him come with me to buy the next year's calendar just so he would know without a shadow of a doubt that I wasn't cheating.

"Did I stump you finally? I did, didn't I?" he asks.

"Jim Plunkett."

"Amazing," he mutters under his breath. "Marry me? Please?"

"But I'm not your type."

"I don't have a type."

"Well, since you put it that way," I say with a laugh. "Meet me at the altar this Saturday at around one o'clock in the afternoon. I'll be the one wearing white."

Dylan sighs dramatically. I can picture him removing his black Ray-Ban eyeglasses and rubbing his temple as if he has the world's worst headache. If I didn't know him well enough, I would think he wore glasses as a fashion statement. The truth is he's blind as a bat but refuses to get the LASIK surgery done because he's terrified of the procedure. Actually, he's terrified of sharp objects near his eyeballs. Can't say that I blame him.

"I can't make it this weekend," he says suddenly.

"To what? Our make-believe wedding?"

"Yes . . . I mean no." He pauses and clears his throat. "No, I mean I can't make the game with you on Friday night. Will you be okay going by yourself?"

This Friday night is the first game of the season for the returning regional champs, Southeast High School Barracudas, and I'll be there to cover it for the *Observer*. And then, of course, I need to write an article on the game and turn it in before we go to press that night for the Sunday morning edition.

"Sure, I'll be fine. Big date?"

His laugh is quick, chopping, and then he says, "Nah, it's a work thing."

Leaning my chair back as far as it will allow, I crane my head to the left slightly to look across the newsroom and straight into Dylan's office. His broad back is currently facing me and he's pacing. Which isn't unusual. In fact, Dylan is a pro at pacing. When we were in college, he left tread marks on what used to be a pretty decent carpet in the newspaper's conference room.

He pivots to walk toward his office door, running a hand through his dark brown hair in what looks like frustration. When he lifts his head finally, his eyes zero in on me from across the room like a beacon. I smile and wave. Dylan waves back with a semi-friendly grin before heading back to his desk and out of my line of vision completely.

"Oh, okay," I say, momentarily confused at his demeanor. "I hope you have fun at your work thing."

"I'll try my hardest," he deadpans, then says a quick good-bye before hanging up.

I stare at the phone in my hand for a moment, as if it sprouted wings, before putting it down on my desk and getting back to work. A short time later, while I'm trolling the usual websites, like Twitter, Facebook, and local high school blogs, my thoughts veer back to my conversation with Dylan. At first I'm concerned I pushed my luck with the whole deadline thing. But no, that's not it. I mean, I'm sure it's a small part of it. But whenever we've had disagreements, we've always bounced back to the easy back-and-forth that has become our trademark. This was . . . I don't know, just different somehow.

I quickly type up my notes and then transfer them to my iPad before stuffing it into my messenger bag. Slinging it over my shoulder, I make a beeline out of the newsroom, trying to ignore the unsettling feeling that has wormed its way into my head. When I reach the glass double doors that lead to the lobby, I turn back around and head straight to Dylan's office instead. His door is closed now and the blinds are drawn. But as I get closer, I can hear him typing away, so I know he's in there.

"He's busy, Ms. Lewis." This comes from Dylan's assistant, Phoebe, who I completely ignore. She's a very play-by-the-rules kind of person who seems like she would cut your throat if she could only find the right opportunity . . . and probably enjoy it too. She worked for the last editor in chief before he retired. And by the looks of her, she's not too far off from retiring herself.

I give her the most humble-as-pie smile I can muster in an effort to placate her. It doesn't work. She peers at me over the eyeglasses she has down the bridge of her nose with a look of disgust. I don't know why the woman hates me so much. I've never done a thing to her. Well, not counting the times I've done exactly what I'm about to do now, because there is no way I can leave without clearing the air with Dylan.

"I'll only take a minute, thanks, Phoebe."

With that, I knock twice on Dylan's door and open it as Phoebe says loudly, in an irritated voice, "I told her you were busy, Mr. Sterling."

Dylan doesn't break the steady stream of typing on his keyboard when he says, "It's okay, Phoebe."

I close the door behind me, then tuck some loose tendrils of hair that have fallen out of the hair clip behind my ears. It's a knee-jerk reaction when I'm nervous, which I happen to be right now. I know I shouldn't be. I mean, Dylan is one of my best friends even though he is my boss. We've managed to not let our friendship interfere with out working relationship, albeit with minor bumps along the way. One of which is that some of our colleagues think that Dylan shows favoritism toward me. Unfortunately, there is not much I can do to dispel that rumor. Wait, that's not true. I'm sure pushing the deadlines doesn't help. But it's not like I'm the only one who does it. I swear, sometimes I wish people would just mind their business and do their jobs instead of assuming I'm getting a free ride. Rest assured, I work my butt off, and Dylan knows it.

"What can I do for you, Katy?"

He still hasn't even so much as glanced in my direction. I walk as if facing a firing squad until I reach the edge of his desk and take a moment to study him in silence.

Dylan has always been more than handsome. His strong jaw and chiseled, rugged features have always made him stand out in a crowd. And with age, he's only grown more into the kind of man that most women would pine for on a daily basis. He's probably one of the smartest people I've ever met. As editors go, he's brilliant and always knows what works and what doesn't in an article. He has a way of looking at every single story objectively, no matter how he feels about the topic. Personally, I find that a man who has looks with intelligence to back them up is irresistible. And Dylan has all of this; the whole package. From the first day we started working together at the college newspaper, it was clear that we would be great friends and get on like two peas in a pod . . . Padawan to Jedi Master. His crisp white dress shirt sleeves are rolled up just past his elbows, because he hates to get even the slightest bit of dirt or grime on them while he's working. The black-and-white-striped tie he started the day with has been loosened, as has the top button of his shirt, which reveals his tan. His usually vibrant green eyes look tired, and the beginnings of a five o'clock shadow are starting to surface.

"I just wanted to apologize if I said anything wrong before. You know, while we were on the phone." I adjust the strap of my messenger bag just to distract myself, waiting for him to acknowledge me with his eyes and feeling like a jerk for barging in.

Finally he stops typing, while I try not to fidget under his withering gaze. I've never been good under scrutiny. And that's exactly what this feels like since he doesn't so much as flinch, blink, or breathe as he looks up at me.

"Dylan?" I ask cautiously.

He seems to snap out of whatever had him in its spell and smiles. It's the kind of smile that I recognize from our many years of friendship, one that says everything is okay between us, and the tight coil of nervous knots in my stomach is undone.

"Everything's fine," he says. "I just have a bunch of stuff going on around here and you know the higher-ups are breathing down my neck again, and then there is that deadline."

He says that last word a little sarcastically. To be honest, I do sometimes forget that Dylan has to answer to a couple of bosses. And their complaints are usually about the newspaper's circulation. We're locally based and have to go against the more well-known paper that covers state and national news too. As a result, every couple of months Dylan is hit with the task of trying to invent new and exciting ways to market our paper and gain readers in addition to all of his day-to-day work. It would stress me out too, and it makes me feel even guiltier for interrupting him today. "So basically just another day at the office."

"Basically." He pulls his hands away from the keyboard and methodically cracks his knuckles one at a time. "Are you heading out already?"

"Yeah. Gonna go to the practice tonight since it's the last one before the game on Friday." I hesitate for a second. "Do you want to come?"

"I wish I could say yes, but . . ."

He motions to the monitor in front of him and I nod in understanding.

"Well, if you need any help or anything, call me, okay? I'll come back in if you want me to."

"Is that your way of saying that you're at my beck and call?" he asks in amusement.

I smile and start to leave. When I reach his door, I turn around and hold the knob only to find him leaning back in his chair while putting his glasses back on.

"Sure, why not?" I say and open the door wide to leave.

As I pass by Phoebe, who gives me a look that leaves no question that she's been sharpening knives while I was in his office, I hear Dylan say, "You might regret that one day, Katy."

CHAPTER TWO

"Y ou look tired. Are you okay?"

Mimi, my other best friend and my roommate, says this to me as she places a container of takeout on the bar in front of me. She's a bartender at Canyon Café, which supplements her income as a fashion designer. She's in design school because, according to her, you can never gain enough knowledge or insight into the world of fashion. And she lives by the very sage advice of one Tim Gunn, her idol: *Make it work.*

While Dylan is my best friend from my college days and I love him to death, he's more like my sounding board because he is a great listener and an all-around good person. And then there is Mimi, my best friend from high school and the best friend to end all best friends. She's the kind of person who you call in the middle of the night to help bury a body. She would show up with a shovel, no questions asked and without the slightest hesitation. She's that loyal.

"I'm fine." I take a sip of my Diet Coke. "The practice just ran a little long and I still have to type up *and* organize all my notes before I go to bed."

"I don't know." She tilts her head to one side and inspects my face more carefully. "There's something else going on. Tell me."

I laugh. Mimi is good at interrogation. Like really, really good. Sometimes I think she missed her calling and should have pursued a career in the FBI. I know I won't last a second under her line of questioning. She can read me like an open book.

"So, come on," she demands. "Tell me all about it. You know you're dying to anyway."

Just then a male customer on the far side of the bar calls out to her. She turns her upper body in his direction and says, "I'll be right there."

As she walks the length of the bar to take his order, she says over her shoulder, "I'll be right back, and then you're gonna spill."

I take the straw from my glass and entertain myself with capturing some soda in it and then draining it back into the glass a few times while she's busy. The incident with Dylan is still bothering me. I thought it was resolved, and he even texted me while I was at the practice to let me know that tomorrow's trivia question was going to stump me. So I honestly don't know why it would still be festering in my head and plainly visible on my face for Mimi to detect.

Mimi sashays back, her small frame encased in tight black jeans and a black fitted tank top, her signature uniform while she's working behind the bar. She hates being objectified, but the tips at the end of the night are always worth it, or so she tells me.

"That guy was a jerk," she says in a hushed voice. "He actually had the nerve to ask me for my number."

I look at the guy in question. He's not bad looking. Kind of tall, which is my best guess since he's sitting in a bar stool, and definitely built but in a not-so-over-the-top way. He has dirty-blond hair and piercing blue eyes that blaze with anticipation while he stares at Mimi's backside.

"He's staring at you," I tell her.

"Of course he is. Have you seen my ass?"

I choke on my soda and start to cough.

For the record, Mimi benefits from what some people would affectionately consider the "J. Lo effect." That might be attributed to her Latin gene pool. Her mother is Cuban and her dad is Puerto Rican.

"Ignore him." She waves a hand by her ear like she is shooing away a fly. "I'm not interested in him anyway."

I lean forward. "And why not? He's kind of hot, Mimi."

"I'm not dating. You already know this, Katy."

"Oh right, I forgot. Why is that again?"

She lifts the drink gun from its holder and proceeds to fill up my glass with more Diet Coke. "Listen, Miss I-Think-I'm-Being-Clever-by-Turning-the-Tables-on-My-Friend, I'm still seeing that guy every so often, and you know I don't do the whole dating around thing." She tops off my glass and then puts the drink gun back in its place before adding, "And no, I'm not going to tell you his name."

"Come on, that's not fair," I whine. "You've been keeping this mystery man under wraps for like three months now."

"And what's your point?"

"My point is by the guidelines set forth in the unofficial best friend handbook, you are required to divulge any and all information pertaining to said mystery man to your best friend." I point to myself and smile. "Who happens to be yours truly."

She squints her caramel brown eyes at me and then leans a little closer. "Nice try, Katy. Don't think I don't remember that you're supposed to tell me what's got you so upset."

"I'm not *that* upset."

"Aha!" She points her index finger in the air. "I knew it!"

"You knew what?"

"I knew you were upset about something," she says with a gratified smile.

I walked right into that one. But instead of spilling my guts about Dylan, I decide to tell her about my scouting from the practice earlier today.

"Well, it's just the Barracudas coach was telling me that Jenkinson—you remember him, right? He's that senior offensive lineman I told you about who's coming off of the injured reserve list. Anyway, Coach is concerned that he won't be ready to play at full—"

Mimi drops her head on the bar and starts to snore out loud. Very loud. So loud that a couple of patrons stop and stare at us.

"Mimi," I say in a low voice, "what the hell?"

She pops her head back up and rubs her eyes as if she just woke up from a catnap. "Oh my God, I'm sorry, Katy. I was just so bored I fell right to sleep while you were talking about sports. Again. For like the millionth time."

"Ha-ha, God you're funny."

"Yeah, I know." She takes the towel from over her shoulder and wipes down the bar quickly. Then she throws it over her shoulder again. "Start talking or else."

Her eyes pierce mine with a glare that I know means I need to take her seriously. One of these days I want to find out what "or else" means. She's petite, so I don't think she could inflict much damage. And I would really like to see her try sometime. I'm pretty sure it would make me laugh in her face.

"Jeez, fine, I'll tell you. It's about Dylan."

Her eyes widen and her mouth morphs into the most ridiculous grin. I should have kept my mouth shut. Mimi is under the delusion that Dylan and I are soul mates. That by some great cosmic misalignment that she cannot ever clearly describe, we are being held captive by our own stupidity and blindness.

"Stop it," I plead in an effort to calm her down. "It's nothing like that."

"You let me be the judge of that."

"Fine."

So I proceed to tell her about what occurred earlier today, careful not to leave out any detail since I know she will pounce on me if I do. Why I entertain her notions about Dylan and me, I have no idea. But it seems to give her a small sense of satisfaction for some reason. As evidenced by the look of wonderment plastered across her face.

"Katy, Katy, Katy," she says with a lilt in her voice. "How many times do I have to tell you? That man is head over heels in love with you. And you're too busy with your silly little football statistics and God knows what else—actually, there isn't anything else, is there?"

"There is something . . . else." My voice falters at the end, much to my dismay.

"Really?" Her eyebrow arches in curiosity. "Tell me what else is there then."

My fingers find the corner of the bar napkin and start to methodically fold it over and over onto itself, until I've made some sort of misshapen origami swan.

Mimi tilts my chin up. "I'm just saying that *this* is all you do. All day, every day, three hundred and sixty-five days of the year. When was the last time you had a real boyfriend or even went out on an actual date? And now that I think about it, when was the last time Dylan had a real girlfriend too? Man, you two are on a serious dry spell. It must be frustrating for him to have *all* that stuff backed up inside of him. You know, I read somewhere recently that men's semen can build—"

"Mimi! I do not want to think about Dylan's semen buildup!"

"Yes you do, you little liar. You just don't want to admit it."

I roll my eyes for what feels like the millionth time in the short while since I've been here. For the record, there is nothing to admit. Dylan and I are fine as we are and always will be. Plus, there are rules in the workplace in this day and age when it comes to dating your subordinate. So I'm sure the thought hasn't even crossed his mind. Not to mention that we're just friends. End of story. And no matter how many times I've tried to convey this to Mimi over the last few years, it goes in one ear and out the other. The worst is when we all hang out here for happy hour, and she tries to ply us with alcohol to, as she puts it, "make things happen." It only makes things uncomfortable for Dylan and me, which of course makes Mimi's day, because she thinks that's just more proof that she's right about us.

"So I'm trying to remember when the last time was for you," she says seriously.

I open my mouth to respond but she beats me to it.

"And no! No way in hell can you say Bailey's name to me. I will not allow it."

Bailey was my boyfriend up until about seven or so months ago. We met at an annual journalism award ceremony and hit it off immediately. He is a columnist at the bigger newspaper in the area and covers major nationwide stories, but he never took what I did seriously because he thought sports was not real news. And it bothered me. A lot. Until my resentment built up and boiled over and I finally told him our relationship had run its course. A tiny part of me hoped that he'd see the error of his ways and tell me that he had made an awful mistake in downplaying what I do for a living. But no such luck. He didn't even deny it. He simply grabbed his jacket from the back of my couch and walked toward the door. When he reached the threshold, he turned around and said, "Stop dreaming, Katy. Nobody's ever going to take you and what you do seriously."

"Look, I'm sorry," Mimi says softly. She covers my hand with hers and gives it a light tap. "It's just I worry about you. You're always so wrapped up in your head and working all the damn time that you never give yourself a moment to unwind."

"What do you call this?" I motion to the bar around us.

"This is you being a good friend and stopping in to say hello because you know I always hook you up with the best chicken quesadillas in all of Fort Lauderdale." She smiles sweetly at me, then folds her arms across her chest.

"Look, Mimi, I—"

Right then, the door to the restaurant opens, and Mimi's eyes narrow. So I pivot in my bar stool to see to whom she's directing her hateful gaze.

I should have known. My brother Simon is still dressed in his officer's uniform with an aura flying off of him that warns anyone who so much as looks in his direction that they shouldn't mess with him.

He walks straight over to us. When he's standing right next to me, Mimi says, "Are there no cats you can be saving from tree limbs right about now?"

I try my hardest not to giggle out loud but fail miserably. Simon gives me a stern look that shuts me up, then directs his attention to Mimi. His glare is enough to frighten me to death, but she just tilts her head as if to say, *Go ahead and give it your best shot.*

Simon, in a very restrained voice, says, "Kiss my ass."

"Shave it first," she responds with a face-splitting smile.

"Okay you two." I try to stop them before it escalates. "Cut it out. I'm not in the mood."

I have no clue why they hate each other so much, but that's the way it's been ever since they met when Mimi and I were in high school and Simon was just starting out in the police academy. The insults never stopped flying, and the sheer amount of "yo momma" jokes that have been tossed between them would even make *Def Comedy Jam* veterans cringe.

"Anyway"—Simon rolls his eyes—"I drove by your place and didn't see your car, so I came by here to check up on you."

"How did you know I was here?"

"I *am* a cop, Katy."

"Are you?" Mimi asks. "'Cause I could have sworn you were just an asshole."

Simon ignores her, which is probably his best move, since Mimi seems as though she has a pocketful of comebacks that she's been waiting to unleash on him for days.

"So if you weren't at work or at the high school tonight, chances were that you would be here. And lo and behold, here you are," he says.

"Okay, I guess." I snatch up my takeout container. "I was just getting ready to go home anyway, so thanks for checking up on me. *Again*."

Simon has made it his life's mission to track my every move, which might have something to do with the fact that our parents were killed by a drunk driver on their way home from a New Year's Eve party when I was a sophomore in high school. As a consequence, he stepped up to the plate and worked two jobs while making sure Jonathan and I were okay through one of the most difficult times of our lives. Not to mention that he did all of this while in the police academy. To this day, I don't know how he managed it all, but I'm grateful nonetheless. He's become that stereotypical overprotective big brother who in the past has scared away potential dates, and he tries to play it off like he's doing me a favor in the process. I don't know when he will ever get the hint that I'm a grown woman and can take care of myself, but I hope it's soon, because I'm so over it by now. And God forbid I voice my opinion on the matter. Because that would start the always fun conversation of how he's my legal guardian—technically, *was* my legal guardian since I've been legal for quite some time, but he conveniently forgets this fact—and how it's his responsibility to watch out for me and make sure I'm safe and sound at all times, day or night.

"Mimi, I'll see you at home later. Be careful, okay?"

She props herself on her elbows and leans forward to kiss me on the cheek. "Don't worry about me, I'll be fine. Go home, heat up that food, and get some rest. We'll continue our conversation tomorrow."

I say good-bye, and Simon follows me to my car as I try my hardest to ignore him, which is impossible to do. He's just over six feet tall and is built like a middle linebacker. He's always been a bit of a health nut, but in the last couple of years his health kick has turned into more of an obsession. But he's not at all vain, even though he's probably propositioned by women daily. This would inflate the ego of most men I know, but not Simon. As protective and intimidating—and annoying—as he comes across, he's actually quite humble and sweet. I do love him very much and always will . . . of course I do, I mean, we *are* family. But I don't need him to constantly be watching over me like a hawk. At some point he has to take a step back and let me live my life.

Right now, though, his protectiveness has reached its limit with me. Especially when I get to my car door and he says, "How many times have I told you to park closer to the entrance or under a streetlight, Katy?"

Under my breath, I mumble, "So many times, I've lost count."

"I heard that," he says. I turn around and give him a hug. "I'm just looking out for you."

He lets go of me and I smile, fully aware that he really does mean well. "I know, Simon. Thanks. I'll talk to you later."

"Sure thing. Good night, Katy."

"Good night."

I toss my bag onto the floor of the passenger side and place my takeout container on the seat. When I pull out of the parking lot, I look in my rearview mirror. At exactly two car lengths behind me, Simon's police cruiser is following me home, as usual.

I sigh out loud and continue driving while thinking some things will never change no matter how much I wish they would.

CHAPTER THREE

"What time did you get home last night?" I ask Mimi as I'm filling up my to-go mug with coffee.

"Um, I don't know exactly, it was late." She yawns, then slowly shuffles her Kermit the Frog slippers against the hardwood floor until she reaches the coffeemaker. Once she's done getting herself a fresh cup of coffee, she shuffles as if on autopilot back to her bedroom and closes the door.

"It was nice talking to you too!" I shout down the hallway.

Muffled, I hear her say, "Ditto. Have a good day at work."

After I've gathered all my essentials and put them in my messenger bag, I check myself in the mirror one last time. I've never been one to get all decked out for work and tend to wear clothes that are practical, much to Mimi's disgust. Same can be said about my hair and makeup. My long, wavy brown hair starts out each day cascading down my back, but by the time I reach the newsroom, it's up in a hair clip with flyaway strands escaping all day long. And as far as makeup, I don't really wear any other than the occasional lip gloss, if you can call ChapStick that.

Today, I'm dressed in a pair of dark wash jeans, a white silk blouse with black polka dots, a black blazer, and black ballet flats. But as soon as I'm in the comfort of my own home, it's sweatpants, tank tops, or T-shirts so old they should have been thrown out years ago.

I'm comfortable in my own skin, as dismaying as it is to other people—Mimi—who wonder why I never get dolled up. A part of me believes in order to be taken seriously I need to look it. However, there is another part of me that wishes I didn't have to waste time even thinking or worrying about my appearance.

When I arrive at the newsroom a half hour or so later, my hair is in its rightful hair clip and I pick up where I left off last night after I got home from the restaurant. Over the next few hours, I research the stats on the visiting high school team and compare them to the Barracudas. Since it's Thursday and there's no practice for either team because it's opening week, I'm able to lose myself in my work. I don't know if it's the numbers or the science of taking all the stats and poring over them carefully, but I could easily spend an entire day doing exactly this.

My desk is on the far end of the newsroom, so it's simple for me to block everyone and everything out. When a light knock on the corner of my desk starts out of the blue, I pop my head up in surprise to find my brother Jonathan smiling at me.

"I called your cell a couple of times but you weren't picking up."

After scanning the desk for my cell, I remember that I never took it out of my bag. Rummaging through it, I find that my cell has three missed calls, two from Jonathan and one from an unknown number, and a text from Dylan that reads:

In 1973, which player became the first punter ever drafted in the first round, 23rd overall to the Raiders?

I quickly text back:

Ray Guy

"So what's up?" I ask Jonathan, placing the phone on my desk, knowing without a doubt that my answer is correct.

He unbuttons his suit jacket and sits on the corner of my desk. "I was just in the neighborhood and wanted to take you out to lunch."

"Is it lunchtime already?"

"It's one thirty in the afternoon. Tell me you've eaten something today other than that." He points to my to-go mug on the far side of my desk.

"Of course I have," I lie.

He leans forward a bit. "Like what, exactly? And don't say Butterscotch Krimpets."

I have a stash of Butterscotch Krimpets in my desk. They are my one and only guilty pleasure and taste sinfully good, especially when dunked in coffee. But today I've been so absorbed in my work that I haven't had one . . . yet. I would have, though, in an hour or so, if Jonathan hadn't shown up when he did and offered to take me to lunch.

"Fine," I say in defeat. "Let's go."

When we approach the elevator my phone buzzes in my pocket. I fish it out, and it shows an unknown number again, and this time whoever or whatever it is left me a voice mail. It's probably a telemarketer. This doubles as my work phone, which means I get bombarded with calls, e-mails, and texts all day, every day, so an unknown number isn't out of the ordinary. Especially when my desk phone's calls have been forwarded to my cell phone since yesterday. Just when I'm about to listen to the message, Dylan's response pops up on my screen.

How did you know that? You looked it up on Google, right?

I don't even bother to answer and instead grin from ear to ear and put the phone back in my pocket. Jonathan notices and says, "What's got you all smiley?"

With a shrug of my shoulders, I say, "Nothing, just Dylan trying to be funny."

We walk to the café across the street, and since the weather is lovely for late September—a perfect not-a-cloud-in-the-sky eighty-one degrees—we opt to eat outside. Once we've ordered, Jonathan begins with the usual questions.

I don't mind his so much as Simon's. Maybe it's because Jonathan has always had a way of talking to me as if I wasn't the baby sister who tagged along with her older brothers, even if that was exactly the case. And when our parents died, he easily slipped into the role of comforter and confidant rather than guardian and warden like Simon did. He's the first person I went to when I decided to become a sports journalist, and his support of me has never faltered.

"Nothing new to report, brother dearest," I say before taking a bite of my cheeseburger. "Simon followed me last night, but that's old news. Like really, really old news. Isn't there something you can do about that for me?"

"I've tried, Katy. Believe me, I've tried."

I nod while I take another bite. Jonathan looks on in disgust as I mix ketchup and mayonnaise together in the perfect concoction to dip my french fries in.

"What? It's delicious." I dip one french fry in the mix and present it to him across the table. "Try it. I guarantee you won't regret it."

He waves a hand dismissively at the slathered fry and shakes his head. "God, no. You know I have an aversion to mayonnaise."

"So what's up with you? How's work?" He's a practicing divorce attorney hoping to make partner one day. He's usually in court, so a lunch date with him is a very welcome treat.

Jonathan wipes his mouth with a napkin before answering. "Good, good. I've got a new case coming up where the soon-to-be ex-wife was cheating on her husband for almost the entire time they were married."

"How long was that?"

"Twelve years."

My mouth drops open. "Really? I mean, the *entire* time? Why did she bother to get married?"

"Who knows," Jonathan says under his breath.

Here's the thing with Jonathan. He's really handsome, extremely sweet, caring, and thoughtful. He would and should make a woman very happy. But his career has tainted how he views relationships. He'd be a great catch for the right woman.

Simon, on the other hand . . . well, who knows what's going with his personal life. Trying to keep tabs on his dating life is harder than trying to find weapons of mass destruction in Iraq.

"How are the Barracudas looking this year?" he asks, obviously wanting to change the subject.

I'm glad for it, because the last thing I want is for him to ask me about any guys I'm not at all dating or could be dating at the moment.

"Really good. I think they're going to go all the way this year. The new coach seems to be picking up where Coach Fraser left off last year."

"That'll be great for our alma mater," he says.

"Yeah," I tell him. "But they're still not as good as when you played for them."

Jonathan was the leading passing quarterback in the entire state of Florida in his senior year of high school. Everyone thought he would pick a football-centered college and continue to flourish at the sport. He was courted by quite a few of them, actually. But he fooled everyone by choosing academics over sports. Not me, though. I always knew that he never intended to play football past high school.

"Thanks." He flashes me a big smile. "I needed that."

"You're welcome."

After we finish eating, we both make a mad dash to grab the bill at the same time. He winks and clucks his tongue at me. "Now, Katy, what kind of big brother would I be if I let you pay when I asked *you* out to lunch?"

"Fine, but next one's on me, okay?"

He reluctantly agrees before leaving a tip on the table and then walking me back across the street to my office. We say our good-byes with tentative plans for him to meet up with me at the game tomorrow night.

Once I'm back at my seat, I take my cell phone out of my pocket and place it on my desk, where I continue to work for the next few hours, oblivious to everything and everyone around me. I don't see or talk to Dylan the rest of the day, so as the day winds down, I decide to see if he wants to meet me at Mimi's work for a couple of drinks later.

But before I call him, I remember the voice mail from earlier. I check and find that I actually have three voice mails. The first is of no importance and the second is from the camera shop, letting me know that the camera I left earlier in the week to be repaired is ready to be picked up, which is perfect timing for tomorrow's game. I have a couple of backup cameras, but this specific camera is my favorite for taking action shots.

I jot down a note to myself to pick up the camera, and then the third message begins to play. I play it again and again. And one more time for good measure, because the caller is unmistakably familiar to me, yet totally foreign at the same time. The fourth time I play it, the hairs on the back of my neck stand up and the ripple of nerves that flows through me is enough to confirm that I'm not imagining things. Because even with the twinge of age added to his voice and the years between us, there is no doubt I'd recognize it anywhere.

"Shadow, I can't believe it's really you. Give me a call back at 786-555-4439."

CHAPTER FOUR

I t can't be.

But nobody other than Conner has ever called me Shadow, so it must be him.

How is it even possible? Where has he been? How did he find me?

I grip the edge of my desk so tightly my fingers feel numb. My breaths start to come out shallow and I can feel a bead of sweat trickling down the back of my neck.

In a brief moment of clarity, I realize that I'm reacting like an absolute lunatic. I mean, it's just a phone call, right? Nothing more, nothing less. People call each other every day and reconnect after years of silence. I mean, that's exactly the point of Facebook. So why should this be anything different?

Katy, I think to myself, *get yourself together.*

Once I begin to feel like everything is settling back to the way it was before I heard his voice . . .

Oh my God, his voice. It sounded so . . . so grown up, mature . . . unmistakably manly. Conner's voice made me feel like I was falling into a blanket and wrapping it around myself until my limbs felt warm and gooey.

Whoa!

Where did that come from? I need to get a grip!

I'm not some lovesick sixteen-year-old girl anymore. *I'm* a grown-up now. I can handle this.

"Okaaay," I say out loud to myself.

"Okay, what?"

I almost jump out of my chair at the sound of Dylan's voice. Swiveling around in my chair, I watch as he leans against my desk. He folds his arms across his chest and stares at me with curiosity brewing in his eyes.

"Is something wrong?" he asks.

"What could be wrong?"

He raises an eyebrow as he looks me over. "I don't know. You're acting weird and talking out loud to yourself, which is a definite sign that you're losing it."

"I'm not losing it." I roll my eyes at him. "Just, um . . . gathering up some notes and stuff. You know? The usual."

I snatch up whatever I can from my desk and chuck it into my messenger bag. I can feel Dylan watching my every move. When I stand and peer up at him, he's trying to stifle a smile as I pull the strap over my head and across my chest.

He steps in closer to me with one hand already slowly reaching for the flap of my messenger bag, and in a low voice, he asks, "May I?"

Before I can say yes or no, and with his eyes never leaving mine, he opens the bag. He pulls out my stapler and places it back on my desk. I'm speechless when he dives back into my bag with his green eyes still pinning me in place and comes out with my Post-it Notes dispenser.

When Dylan's gaze breaks away from mine for a moment to calmly place the dispenser back in its rightful place on my desk, I feel a blush creeping up my neck until my cheeks are burning with embarrassment.

"Obviously, you're not losing it," he says, still smiling and turning his attention back to me again. "Not even a little bit, huh?"

I tug some loose hair behind my ear and then tilt my head to the side. "I got carried away, I guess."

He opens his mouth to say something but nothing comes out. His lips freeze mid-word as his hands go into his pants pockets and he takes a step back at the same time. I can tell that what he says next isn't what he originally intended by the mask that smoothly slips back into place, wiping the smile almost clean from his face.

"If you say so, Katy."

"I do," I rattle off like an idiot with a huge fake grin. "I say so. I'm A-OK, I promise."

Dylan nods, then asks, "Are you heading over to Mimi's for a drink?"

Then I remember that I was going to invite him to meet me there as an olive branch for skating so close to the deadline yesterday, but after Conner's call, I'm reeling. I couldn't bear to be around Mimi, much less Dylan, while I'm contemplating Conner and his voice mail and all that it entails.

"No. I'm going home. Want to make it an early night tonight. You know, with tomorrow being the big game and all."

"Sure. Sounds good," he says. "I'll see you tomorrow then."

Dylan turns on his heel and weaves ever so efficiently through the throng of desks and general madness of the newsroom. When he reaches his office, he closes the door behind him. The sound of his door closing literally snaps me back into action.

To do what, exactly, I have no idea whatsoever.

Probably go home and brood over Conner and that last meeting of ours before he left. Of course I have thought about him over the years; we were best friends, so it's only natural. Sometimes all it takes is a song or something similarly cheesy to trigger a memory of him and how much I wished things had gone differently between us. Alas, it was never in the cards for us, because he never saw me as anything other than a friend. His shadow.

But now . . .

"Now what?" I say out loud to myself while walking through the lobby.

"Now what, what, Katy?" Jamie, the perky blonde receptionist, asks me.

She startles me, and I stop walking long enough to turn to face her. "Oh, nothing. Just thinking out loud about an article."

Jamie looks at me with sympathy. "You poor thing. You always look so stressed. Go home and take a long, hot bath with some candles and a glass of wine. That does the trick for me when I'm feeling like that."

Since when do I *always* look stressed? And how come nobody's ever bothered to let me in on that tidbit of information until now? I know I can come across as maybe a little busy and in my own head sometimes, but that doesn't necessarily mean I'm stressed. The newsroom can be a cutthroat environment, so there might not be time during the day to play catch-up with everyone and see how they're doing. Then again, I don't have many acquaintances here that I would confide in due to the fact that most people think I have an in with the boss.

"I'll be fine." I start walking toward the elevator doors again and then add as an afterthought, "Thanks for the advice, Jamie. Good night, and have a great weekend."

"You too."

Once I start driving home, I plug my phone into the audio jack and do the one thing that could possibly place me in the realm of definitely losing it, like Dylan suggested earlier—I play Conner's voice mail through the speakers of my car in stereo surround sound. His voice, I've learned after listening to the message another three times on the drive home, sounds hopeful and expectant and something else I can't quite put my finger on.

While parked at my apartment complex, I crane my neck and listen to the message one last time to try and pinpoint more inflections in his voice when the phone rings, scaring me to death. That might be because it's Mimi's special ringtone of Madonna's "Vogue" blaring through my speakers.

She changes the ringtone every so often, and I have no idea when or why she does it. After the first couple of times, I changed my phone's passcode, but the little sneak will catch me over my shoulder when I'm engrossed in something and memorize it so that she can do her handiwork without my knowledge. The worst was when she changed the ringtone to "Milkshake" by Kelis and proceeded to call me, knowing full well I was at a very important staff meeting.

I'm still trying to live that day down. Unsuccessfully, I might add.

"Are you coming by tonight?" she asks by way of hello.

"Not tonight."

"And why not?"

"Just not feeling up to it. Gonna get some rest instead. It's a big day tomorrow, season opener and—"

"Please. Stop. Say no more," she says, already bored to death. "Okay then, I'll catch up with you later or tomorrow, depending on what time I get home tonight."

Once she says good-bye, I don't torture myself any further and unplug the phone from the audio jack. A glance at the clock in the dashboard tells me I've been sitting in the parking lot for just over ten minutes. Not healthy behavior in the slightest.

I walk toward the apartment door with sweat already accumulating on the back of my neck from the early evening humidity. I'd like to think that it's because of the weather, but it's much more than that. But why am I feeling anxious and nervous and completely unsure of what I'm supposed to say to him? That is, if I actually call him back.

Who am I kidding?

Of course I'm going to call him back.

Still, how would the conversation go?

Hi, Conner! Oh yeah, can we forget the very last thing I ever said to you? That would be great, thanks!

"Not likely," I mumble under my breath as I stalk closer to my apartment.

A wall of cool air blasts me when I finally swing the door open. I relish the central air conditioning while dropping my things on the couch and make a beeline over to the kitchen. Taking Jamie's advice, I uncork a bottle of already chilled wine and pour myself a tall glass. Mimi would probably throw a parade if she could see me now, since I don't drink this quickly after I'm home from work, if at all. I enjoy the taste on my lips before taking a large, unladylike sip. *God, that's good.* Not that alcohol can cure any problem, but right now, I desperately need something to calm my nerves.

Leaning against the kitchen counter for a few minutes, I let the wine seep into my bloodstream while I stretch my neck and luxuriate in the feel of it coursing through my veins. Then, I'm off, knowing full well that what I do next can only be chalked up to my already frazzled state. The funny part is that I'm aware of the wrongness of it all as I'm walking toward my bedroom with my wineglass in one hand—clutching it for dear life is more like it—and the mostly full bottle of wine in the other.

I crouch down until I'm on my knees by the foot of my bed. When I lift one corner of the sky-blue-and-chocolate-flower-patterned comforter to the side, the plain white storage box is sitting in its familiar place, tucked safely away from prying eyes. Mine, in particular.

I can count on one hand the times I've pulled it out to relive my past. The last time was a couple of years ago on the anniversary of my parents' death. Once I finished looking over the pictures and letters, knickknacks, and other odds and ends, I put the box back underneath my bed thinking that it would be the last time, that I could somehow move on and not go back to it. However, something always seems to trigger the urge to pull it out and dredge up the other kinds of memories, the not-so-good kind; the kind that I want to revel in right now no matter how awful it will be.

After I drag the box toward me, I sit on the floor and place it on my lap. I take one last long drink from my wineglass and immediately decide that I need a refill. So I top off my glass and then gather up the courage to open the storage box.

The scent of lavender immediately envelops me, and a smile tugs at the corners of my mouth. My mom used to buy bundles of it to display in my childhood home. The piney, floral, and slightly camphoraceous scent always tickles my nose, reminding me of her and how'd she spend hours arranging them just so.

I gingerly pick up the dried sprigs and place them on the floor beside me, careful not to damage them in any way. Then I start rifling through the box with more determination than I thought I had in me.

When I reach the very bottom of the box, I see it. The letter.

It's still folded neatly, as if it was never opened. But it was, only once, by the person whose name appears on it in my handwriting: Conner.

As I pull it out from its secure hiding spot underneath all my other treasured memories, I think about a girl who was lovesick and unsure, afraid and thrilled, and completely different from whom I am today. But as I sit here with it in my hands again after all these years, I'm her again: the sixteen-year-old girl who thought Conner hung the moon.

"God, I was so stupid."

A chuckle escapes me, but it sounds forced to my own ears. Finally, I move the box off of my lap and lay the letter faceup in its place. It stares back at me, egging me on to open it. And I do. And when I read it now, years later, feeling everything the sixteen-year-old me was feeling when she wrote it, I still wish that I never wrote it in the first place.

CHAPTER FIVE

A woman's voice speaking in an almost hush is the first thing I notice the next morning, but I can't make out what she says clearly.

Maybe it's my own? No, that can't be right since my tongue feels like it's shellacked to the roof of my mouth, and my head feels as if it will split open at any moment if I move it too swiftly. In hindsight, drinking almost the entire bottle of wine last night was probably not the wisest decision I've ever made.

The woman's voice goes on speaking, distracting me for a moment.

I keep my eyes closed, thinking I'm just hovering in a dreamlike state, that place in between two worlds where you want to continue sleeping but know that it won't last for very much longer. That's when the woman's voice breaks through the veil of sleep again for good.

"I wish when you looked at me that you saw somebody different. Because I want to be so much more to you than a friend, Conner. I have for such a long time."

My eyes fly open when I recognize the voice and what she's reading. I knife up in my bed, spotting her sitting casually at the far edge and pointing a finger at me in mock accusation.

"Girl, you've been seriously holding out on me. Who the hell is Conner?"

"Mimi!" I yell and instantly regret it when it feels like my head almost explodes off my shoulders.

Spotting the letter in her hand, I lean forward and try to yank it back, but she stands up and it's out of my grasp. She immediately goes back to reading it aloud.

"I want you to be my first kiss and more."

Mimi pauses and fans herself with the letter. "Damn, no beating around the bush for you, huh?"

I cover my face with my hands and groan. "Please stop reading that."

"Are you kidding? This is like the best letter I've ever read in my entire life."

She starts to pace at the foot of my bed and recites the last two sentences, which I've already committed to memory.

"Please give me a chance to prove to you that I'm not a little girl anymore. I love you, Conner, I always will."

I feel the mattress shift, and as I uncover my eyes to sneak a peek at her, she's sitting at the edge of the bed again with a smug smile on her face.

"Start talking. Now," she says.

Before I respond, I quickly reach forward and pull the letter out of her hand. Once I've folded it back to the way it was before last night, I tuck it underneath my pillow for safe keeping while Mimi's still in my room. There is no way I could possibly hide it in its normal spot while she's in here. Because knowing her, she'll be rummaging through all my things, and I'll never hear the end of it.

"Well, first of all," I say as calmly and quietly as possible so as to not further antagonize my headache, "why are you snooping through my things?"

"I wouldn't call it snooping."

"Oh really? Then what would you call it, exactly?"

She smacks her lips together, her eyes going as wide as saucers, and then says, "It was on your chest, faceup, and begging for me to read it."

My face contorts as I try to remember how it ended up like that. Then I recall the wine from last night and how I'm still wearing my clothes from work yesterday, shoes and all. I must have passed out while I was reading it at some point and . . .

"Wait, why were you in here anyway?"

She sighs and flops down on her back across the foot of my bed. "I was worried about you."

"Pfft, please," I mutter and go to rub my temples gingerly.

"No, really," she says, stretching her arms above her head as if she hadn't a care in the world. "You hadn't gotten up to get your morning coffee—you *always* beat me to the morning coffee." She rolls over and props herself on her elbows to face me. "Anyway, when I noticed it wasn't even made yet, I came to your room and knocked. You didn't answer, and I got worried so I opened the door. I noticed the letter on your chest, grabbed it, and started reading. So there you have it, mystery solved. Now tell me about this Conner fellow and how I've never heard of him until now. Oh, and make sure you include the part where you wanted to give him your V card since you told me you gave that away to that poor schlub on prom night who followed you around like a lost puppy dog our entire senior year."

I throw my legs over the side of the bed and plant my feet on the hardwood floor. "There's nothing to tell, Mimi. Please just leave it alone. And Neil wasn't a schlub."

Neil Martin was a semi-friend of mine who also worked on the high school newspaper. And he was the only boy who asked me to prom. He was my first, and it was as awful and awkward as one could imagine, especially when I didn't really like him in that way and was only trying to relieve myself of the "affliction," as Mimi used to call it back then.

He *was* kind of a schlub, now that I think about it. Poor Neil.

"Ha! Nice try. If you know anything about me, then you must know that there is no way in hell I'm going to forget about that." She points to the now safely hidden letter underneath my pillow. "Or . . . hmm . . ."

My head snaps to look over my shoulder at her again as she's tapping an electric blue, perfectly manicured fingernail against her teeth.

"Or what?" I ask.

"Or, I could just ask Simon about Conner. He probably knows about him, right?"

"Why would you ask Simon anything? Don't you two hate each other?"

She shrugs her shoulder and sits up. "Yeah, but I'd take one for the team just to find out about this Conner you obviously were dying to f—"

"Stop! I wasn't dying to . . ." I wave my hand frantically in front of me like I'm swatting a fly. "You know, do *that*. It's complicated."

"Let me be the judge of how complicated your torrid affair with Conner was."

I can't help it. I laugh. Torrid would be the very last word I would ever choose to describe our relationship. Even using the word "relationship" makes me uneasy. Friends, yes. Definitely friends. But a relationship? And a torrid one at that? I don't think so.

Mimi scoots over until she's sitting next to me on the side of the bed. She bumps my shoulder and says, "Katy, you're kind of freaking me out."

I sigh and give in to her. I tell her the abbreviated version, ending up at his random phone call yesterday and my tiny break with reality last night when I decided to drink and read the letter I'd written him again after years of keeping it hidden like a bad secret. Thankfully, she doesn't interrupt once or add any colorful commentary, even though I know she's probably dying to. I guess that's why we're still best friends after all these years; she knows when I need her to just be there for me and vice versa. Mimi can be a pain in the ass, opinionated, and moody, but she's also incredibly thoughtful and caring. I try to hang on to that instead of dwelling on the fact that she purposely read the letter that I obviously didn't want anyone else to ever read in this lifetime or the next.

When I finish, she asks, "Why didn't you ever tell me about him when we met in high school?"

"I don't know," I say.

But that's not true and she knows it. I met Mimi shortly after my parents died. At the time the school's counselor recommended to my brothers that I ease my way back into the curriculum instead of just going for broke on my first day back. So they paired me up with another student who would help me by going over class notes and previous assignments and general social reacclimatization. That student was Mimi. And we've been inseparable ever since.

"Okay, so you neglected to tell me about him back then. Not a big deal. You're forgiven." Mimi's eyes light up and then she says, "But now—"

"Now what?" I immediately regret saying this out loud. "You know what? Forget I asked."

"Of course there is a now what." She stands up and plants both hands on her hips. "Now, you have me at your disposal to help you catch him."

I laugh as I brush my hair off my face to look up at her. "I'm not going to try and catch him, Mimi. I mean, it's been years since we've seen each other; we've both changed a lot since then. Not to mention he's probably married or has a girlfriend or something. And I'm not even interested in him like that anymore."

"Sure you aren't."

"It's true." I slowly stand up, still feeling off-kilter. "I'm not."

"You do realize you drank an entire bottle of wine last night and—"

I hold my hand up to stop her. "For the record, I did not drink an entire bottle of wine."

"Fine. You didn't drink an *entire* bottle of wine." Mimi leans against my dresser and smiles. "You drank an almost-full-to-the-brim bottle of wine."

I don't even bother to correct her, which she takes as a sign that I want to continue this conversation, when in fact I want nothing more than to pretend yesterday never happened.

"So you're drunk here. All alone, I might add," she says as if that was scandalous. "Then you pull this letter out from God knows where and spend the rest of your drunk time pining over this dude, Conner."

I run my hands through my hair in frustration. Deciding that I must be the one to nip this conversation in the bud, I grab my robe from the back of my closet door and start walking to the bathroom to take a shower.

"I mean, who does that?" Mimi asks as she follows me. "If that's not a sign that there is some kind of unrequited puppy love bullshit between you two, then I don't know what is."

When I reach the bathroom, I turn around swiftly, and she almost runs right into me. "If you don't mind," I say quietly, "I'd like to take a shower in peace and quiet."

She leans against the door frame. "Actually, yeah, I do mind."

I tilt my head to the side. "You do, huh?"

"We should talk about this, Katy. I want to help."

Mimi's smile widens and her eyes dance with excitement at the prospect. So I do the one thing I know without question will douse her desire to keep this conversation going.

"You know what?" I ask innocently, and she gives a quick shake of her head. "I do need your help with something."

She claps her hands together. "What?!"

"I could use some help tonight at the game. You know, like helping with stats and maybe some pictures and note taking. Kind of like a tag team."

"I'd rather stick needles in my eyes."

I smile. "Well, now you know how I feel."

She steps back long enough for me to close the door and lock it. From behind it, she shouts, "That's not fair!"

I ignore her and take my shower, standing underneath the hot water for a good twenty minutes. It helps to clear my head tremendously and does wonders for my hangover. Before long, I'm dressed and grabbing my morning cup of coffee from the kitchen.

And that is when the wind is knocked right out of my sails. Because as I'm bringing the coffee mug to my lips, my cell phone rings from inside my messenger bag. The problem is that Mimi hears it too. Her ears prick up like a German shepherd's at the sound. We then stare at each other over the rim of our respective mugs, waiting to see who's going to move first. Mimi's mouth curling up in a devilish grin gives her away, so I casually put my mug down and make my move. She's quick on my heels and jumps over the back of the couch to beat me to it.

"Don't you dare," I say in my most deadly voice.

With a devious smile on her lips, she fishes my cell phone out anyway and quickly answers it.

"Hello," she says into the phone, her eyes glinting with mischief. "Oh no, this isn't Katy. This is her amazing and totally awesome best friend and roommate, Mimi, at your service." She stops herself long enough to stare back at me in defiance before adding as an afterthought, "It's nice to meet you too, Conner."

I mute-yell at her and wave my arms to get her to stop as if I'm signaling a jet to a safe landing on a runway. But she just keeps right on going as if I wasn't even there, as if this is something she does every single day of her life. As if she doesn't even realize how absolutely nuts she is.

"Actually, she's kind of tied up at the moment and probably will be most of the day. But she will be stopping by my job later tonight."

I inch up closer to her as my face flames red in anger, and she immediately puts a hand up to stop me. "It's called Canyon Café."

"Oh my God, please hang up," I whisper in between clenched teeth.

"Well, I'm a fashion designer by day and bartender by night. You know how it is . . . a girl's gotta do what a girl's gotta do to make the rent." She tosses her head back and laughs at whatever he says, then blurts out, "So, are you single?"

That's it. I'm going to kill her.

She peers up at me and must see that I've reached my limit, because all of a sudden she looks panicked.

"Yeah, she's just really busy right now, Conner," Mimi says.

My hands lunge forward. Whether it's to choke Mimi or bat the phone away from her ear, I'm not sure. She starts walking backward toward the kitchen again, talking a mile a minute on the phone. "Yes, that's right. It's called the Canyon Café, and she'll be there at nine thirty tonight."

The blood drains from my face and my stomach lurches as she gives me a quick thumbs-up and finally says good-bye to Conner. She presses a button on my phone and then hands it back to me.

When I stand there frozen for a second or two, she says, "He's single."

"I can't believe you just did that to me." I cover my face with my hands and then mumble, "And I can't believe you asked him if he was single."

Mimi appears unfazed and undeterred. If anything, she looks as if she thinks she just did me the world's biggest favor. She proves me right by saying with a huge smile and a wink, "You're welcome."

CHAPTER SIX

Usually, I'm extremely focused while I'm working. For example, tonight, the opening game of the Barracudas' season, I should be attuned to every play on the field from the moment the referee's whistle blows in the first quarter until the very end.

But I'm not.

My thoughts are all over the place. I can barely concentrate on the game as I try to push out of my head the idea of seeing Conner in . . . ? I glance at my watch to confirm how much time I have. Christ! I have less than three hours.

All right, I need to get my butt in gear and actually try to get some work done. I've never ever missed a deadline and I'm not about to let this keep me from making one. I start by taking my camera out of my bag and snapping a few pictures, which seems to help to get me back on track, so I decide to continue taking pictures by walking to the far side of the field and closer to the goal line, where the Barracudas are in the red zone again.

Once I'm stationed there and the play is called dead by the referee, I hear a familiar voice standing right next to me.

"They look really good. Just like you said they would."

I smile behind the lens and say, "I told you they'd be amazing this year."

I pull the camera away from my face to look at Jonathan, who's dressed casually and looks more relaxed than I've seen him in a very long time. Too long.

"Do you need help with anything?"

"No." I put the camera back in my bag for the moment. "Just wanted to take some shots before they scored."

He nods and folds his arms across his chest. And the look of pure bliss on his face as he watches the action play out on the field helps me to regain the focus I was severely lacking.

See, when you get down to it, football is like a well-choreographed ballet. Albeit with violent hits, grunts and groans, and cheers from the sea of people on the aluminum benches on either side. Because a player can run with the grace and speed of a gazelle down the field while the ball sails in the air in a tight spiral to his awaiting, outstretched arms. And then the chase ensues with finesse and strength displayed by both teams. No matter the outcome, one team chants victory as the other hangs their heads in disappointment. It's beautiful and at times tragic, and I love every single second of it.

Before long, the game is over and the Barracudas, as I predicted, win handily with a final score of 45–14. As I'm finishing up my notes, Jonathan says a quick good-bye and lets me know that he'll catch up with me later in the week. I head on over to the Barracudas' new head coach for a quick interview. I also want a few words with their star wide receiver, who I'm sure is going to be famous one day if he stays healthy. He's got the work ethic, the grades, and the support system all in place to make it to the big time. But more than anything, he has a raw talent and hunger for the game unlike anything I've ever seen before. He is a true force to be reckoned with on the field, and to witness talent like that blossom over the last three years is a privilege, as far as I'm concerned.

When I get through the throng of parents and other local sports journalists as well as the Barracudas' school reporter, my phone is ready to record so that I can ask the head coach a question or two.

"Coach Monroe, was there a key play that made the game a win for you?"

The coach swivels his head around to see me waiting with phone in hand for his sound bite. His smile turns almost sickly sweet, and in a condescending voice, he says, "Little lady, it's something called a touchdown."

While he chuckles, my face is an unflappable mask as the blood boils in my veins. This is certainly not the first time I've encountered a man who thinks I'm just some hapless girl who can easily be dismissed, and it certainly won't be the last. But I still struggle with the fact that being accepted will never be easy as a woman in this field. No matter how many times I prove to others that I know what I'm talking about, people like Coach Monroe will always be there to remind me that I have to keep fighting.

As much as I try not to let it show that his answer bothers me, I decide to ask a follow-up question with a hint of warning behind it so he'll know that I'm not to be treated like this in the future. "Obviously the touchdowns, but I want to know if there was a specific play that turned the game around for you and the team? For example, finally realizing at the start of the second half that the Knights consistently lined up in a nickel defense. And as a result, drawing them off the line to get that big offsides penalty late in the third quarter to put the Barracudas in the red zone and ultimately scoring to take the lead for good?"

His smug smile was replaced by a slightly shocked expression, followed by a quick gulp of air. I can tell that he's trying to reconcile the "little lady" image he sees in front of him with the fact that she knows what the hell she's talking about. And when Coach Monroe struggles to respond, I suppress the laughter bubbling in my throat by coughing a little.

"Excuse me," I tell him, clearing my throat one more time and putting the phone closer to his mouth. "Can you please say that again?"

My face is neutral regardless of the triumph I feel while I record his answer, which confirms my suspicions: that the Barracudas did in fact draw that penalty on purpose to put them in scoring position.

When I draw back my phone from his mouth, I say, "Thank you, Coach."

"You're welcome, Ms. . . . ? I'm sorry, I didn't catch your name."

"Ms. Lewis, from the *Florida Observer*," I say as I'm already backing away from the group of people surrounding him. "I'll be in touch if I need anything else from you."

And with that, I separate myself from the remaining crowd *and* from the moment. Because I don't want what happened to ruin the rest of my night. I've set him straight, and going forward he will treat me with the respect I deserve . . . hopefully. If not, well, I'll figure something out, I'm sure. By this time the players have left, including the star receiver I was hoping to interview, which sucks, so while I'm still in my work zone and waiting for the parking lot to clear out a bit, I sit on the sideline bench so that I can begin typing on my iPad the actual article that I have to submit by midnight. Articles on the Barracudas don't take me that long to do, usually; it's the perfecting part that puts me in the precarious right-up-to-edge-of-my-deadline position. My cell phone starts to vibrate, but I ignore it since I'm in the midst of working. When it rings again almost immediately, I decide to answer.

"It's almost ten o'clock, where the hell are you?" Mimi whisper-yells into my ear.

"I—"

"Wait. Don't answer that. Just tell me that you're on your way here right now."

I look up to find that only the officiating crew is left on the field and then check behind me to see that the parking lot has a handful of cars left.

"Um, yeah, I was just leaving." After I gather up my belongings, I start walking toward my car, which Simon would be so pleased to learn is parked underneath a streetlight.

Mimi's voice is so quiet that I can barely make out what she says next. "Okay, because this Conner guy is here, I think."

I stop in my tracks just a few feet away from my car. "What? Oh my God, he really showed up?"

"That's the thing. I don't have a goddamn clue what he looks like, but I think this guy must be him."

"Why do you think it's him then?" I regain my composure long enough to walk the rest of the distance to my car and unlock the door. "What does he look like?"

"Well, for one, he's gorgeous," she says. "Kind of tall, built, light brown hair, and ridiculously perfect hazel eyes. I mean, from where I'm standing they look like they could also be green, I guess, I don't know."

"That doesn't prove anything," I say, even though I'm fairly certain she's right.

"And two," Mimi adds, ignoring me. "He arrived just before nine thirty and has been watching the front door like a hawk every time it swings open."

The nerves in my stomach start to bubble, and I swear my feet and arms go numb. Which I'm pretty sure are the beginning signs of an anxiety attack, which is making it more difficult to operate my car. I have to take a deep breath to calm my nerves when my right foot steps on the gas pedal to start driving the ten or so minutes from here to Mimi's job.

"Okay, I'll be there in a few minutes. Let me get off the phone so I can concentrate on the road. And by the way, yes, I'm still mad at you for doing this."

"Yeah, yeah, yeah. Just hurry up," she whispers.

Of course the drive over to the restaurant takes me a little longer than expected since I hit every single red light on the way. This isn't necessarily a bad thing, because it allows me a few extra minutes to gather my thoughts. For instance, where has he been, what has he been doing, and finally, will he bring up the letter and how we left things between us?

If he does, I've already decided that I'll play it off like it was all just some silly little crush. Because that's exactly what it was. I'm older, wiser, and not at all interested in pursuing anything with anyone right now in my life anyway.

As if.

"Jeez," I mumble to myself and turn into the parking lot of Canyon Café. When did my life turn into something that requires Cher Horowitz–type commentary?

I flip down the visor to look at myself in the mirror. Tucking some flyaway strands of hair behind my ears, I look surprisingly calm even though my brain is off flying in a million different directions. But at least I have regained the feeling in my extremities, so I have that going for me, if all else fails.

Inside the restaurant, I see Emily, the hostess, first. She says a quick hello, and then I look to my left to scope out the bar area. Mimi's attention is focused on a couple of women at the far end of the bar, so her back's turned to me. There are a few other patrons here and there, which is the norm for a Friday night. I coast over every male customer until my eyes stop on one particular guy . . . no, that's not right . . . a man. A very good-looking, fully grown-to-perfection Conner with his gorgeous hazel eyes staring right back at me. The corners of his mouth tip up in a warm, inviting smile when he recognizes me.

My feet are stuck to the floor, but that's of no consequence, since he stands up from his bar stool and looks like he's going to walk over to me. I watch in rapt attention as he puts his beer bottle on the bar, then wipes his hands on his jeans. When he does this, his biceps flex underneath his plain white T-shirt, hinting at the muscular body that has developed really well since we last saw each other. His wavy brown hair, which seems lighter than what I remember, looks like it needs a trim from the way the ends flip up a little. Then again, it always seemed as if it needed a trim, but that look always worked for him.

When Conner is finally standing within arm's reach, I almost don't believe that it's really him. But when that smile turns into the very familiar smirk from my past that I came to love and know well, there's no doubt it is.

"Katy," he says.

"Conner."

He hesitates for a moment before stepping forward and wrapping his arms around me in a big hug. As I bring my arms up to reciprocate, he tilts his head a fraction so he can place a friendly, quick kiss on my cheek. My eyes close when I feel him squeezing me tighter, like he doesn't want to let me go. Or maybe it's just my overactive imagination where he's concerned.

That's when I hear him say in a low voice, "It's been too long, Shadow."

And just like that, I'm transported to that day on the playground so many years ago when we first met.

CHAPTER SEVEN

Fourteen years ago . . .

The unfortunate thing about being a girl with two older brothers and living in a neighborhood with no other girls around your age is that you're predestined to be a tomboy. If I wanted to go out and play, or do anything for that matter, I was a slave to whatever my brothers and their friends wanted to do. And I followed them around like a lost puppy dog, never quite knowing my place, always feeling somewhat out of the loop on everything, and certain that I was the butt of all their jokes.

So there I was on the top of the slide, feeling too old to get away with using it to begin with. My long legs were impatiently kicking out in front of me, looking for purchase on the slippery surface before gripping the sides, and with one final push, I let go. I slid down and came to a body-jarring stop before tumbling onto the ground, a move I had been perfecting over the course of the summer that saved me many a scratched or bruised knee. Instead of climbing back up the way I came, though, I stayed at the bottom of the slide, dragging my feet through the sand to make silly swirls and figure eights until my oldest brother, Simon, yelled out my name.

By now, my brothers had gathered a mostly familiar crew of boys from the playground, and they were all in a circle formation with a light buzz of energy floating in the air around them, as if they were going to perform some sort of religious ritual instead of throwing the pigskin around for an hour or two.

"Everyone," Simon announced when I reached his side. "Katy's my pick for running back."

A low rumble of disapproval could be heard from all the other boys. This wasn't the first time that I'd experienced this, so I was more than used to it. Instead of being intimidated, though, which was exactly how an eleven-year-old girl should feel when facing the firing squad of older boys, I stood there defiant. My hand was on my hip and the tiny chip on my shoulder was growing by the second as I looked at all of their faces, which didn't hide at all how unhappy they were that a girl was going to be playing with them.

All except for one unfamiliar face.

He stood off to the side, partially obscured by another boy, but not enough that I didn't detect the smirk on his mouth. And he was beautiful. The most beautiful boy I had ever seen in all my life, which at eleven years old wasn't saying much. But to me, he was perfect.

He had chestnut brown hair that was in need of a trim because of the way the ends flipped up underneath the snug New York Mets baseball cap he was wearing. His eyes glistened in the sunlight: a warm hazel that made my heart melt. But it was that look, the one that said to me that he thought I wasn't good enough to play with them, that did me in.

This was the first time I had ever seen him at the playground.

I made sure to pay attention when he introduced himself. "Conner," he said, his voice like a melody playing just for me. And for the very first time, I was nervous of looking like a fool in front of all these boys. Well, not all of them, just him, really.

Before I knew it, a quarter was tossed, teams were lined up, and Simon was handing off the football into my eager hands as someone from the other team yelled out, "One Mississippi."

By "two Mississippi" I was darting around the left side of the makeshift offensive line, my small feet running as if my life depended on it, down the sideline and clutching the ball to my chest like it was the Holy Grail. By "three Mississippi" I had made it halfway to the end zone and could see no opposition. By "four Mississippi" I heard the other team groaning and my team cheering me on to score a touchdown.

I didn't get to hear "five Mississippi."

That was because I had been tackled out of nowhere and was lying flat on my back.

At first, the shock of landing so hard caused tears to well up in my eyes. I squeezed them tightly shut and willed myself not to cry. Because even though I was obviously a girl, I didn't want to be "like a girl" in front of all them. Once I had that under control, I noticed that it was eerily quiet. This playground that was usually bursting at the seams with activity had come to a complete halt. Then I registered a heavy weight across my legs, which was keeping me tethered to the ground. Its grip on me started to loosen, and that's when I sat up and looked at what—or rather, who—had its hold on me.

Conner.

He was beaming with a smile as he let me go completely and stood up. It made his already beautiful face almost angelic to me. I couldn't help myself; I goofily smiled back. And that's when I knew I was in trouble.

A second later and ruining this very perfect moment, Jonathan arrived by my side, crouching down to make sure I was okay by checking and rechecking every one of my limbs until I shooed him away and reassured him that I was fine. Then Simon appeared. He stepped in front of Conner and shoved him hard until he fell to the ground, the smile now wiped clean from his face.

If it had been anybody else, I probably would have let my brother continue to berate him in front of everyone. To this day, I don't know if it was because Conner played by the actual rules and tackled me rather than abiding by some unspoken rule that I was not to be touched. Or maybe it was all as simple as just the way he smiled at me afterward or the look on his face when I first noticed him. Whatever it was, I knew I didn't want Simon to hurt him.

"Stop it!" I yelled. "Leave him alone!"

I stood up and brushed the dirt from my backside, then gathered up the courage to step in front of Simon.

"Get out of here, Katy," he said. "I'll handle it."

He tried to sidestep me but I blocked him again.

"He was just playing the game," I said. "He didn't do anything wrong."

"Are you serious? He could have really hurt you and you're sticking up for him?" he asked incredulously.

I kept my chin up and stood my ground once more. This was going to be the one time that my brothers were not going to get their way, if I had anything to say about it.

"But I'm not hurt. The tackle was fair and square. And I'm fine. Honest."

Simon looked over my shoulder to Conner and said to him, "You're done. Go home."

Before Simon turned around to walk back on the field, I said, "Then I'm not playing anymore either."

"Katy, don't be stupid."

"You're the one being stupid."

There was a collective "ooh" from the crowd that had formed around us. They had never heard me talk back to either brother, and I found myself gaining more confidence with every uncomfortable second that passed. Simon gave Conner one last disgusted glance, then turned on his heel as the crowd parted to let him walk away.

"Suit yourself," he muttered under his breath.

Not too long after that, the other boys followed him back onto the field. No surprise there. Wherever Simon went, people just naturally followed.

"Are you sure you're all right?" Jonathan asked, walking backward to join the rest of the boys.

I nodded and gave him a reassuring smile, which seemed to appease him since he left me and Conner alone.

Turning around, I immediately put my hand out to help him up.

"I didn't need your help, you know," he said and refused my out-stretched hand.

"I know you didn't."

"Then why did you do that?"

He was standing up by now. The baseball hat had been pushed back farther on his head, revealing more of his handsome face. It was so difficult to get my mouth to actually move and form words. They were all bottled up in my throat as I stared at him up close, taking in every detail of his features and committing them to memory.

"Never mind," he said and started to leave.

I couldn't let him get away, so I ran up behind him until we both settled for walking side by side at the same pace. To his credit, he didn't tell me to go away, nor did he walk any faster to lose me. Instead, he looked over at me and smiled shyly before quickly looking ahead again.

When we reached the entrance to the park, he said, *"Listen, I'm sorry that I was mean to you before."* He jerked a thumb behind him toward where the other boys were playing again. *"Thanks for sticking up for me back there."*

"That's okay," I said.

"You know, you're pretty fast . . . for a girl."

I beamed with a smile from ear to ear from his praise. *"Thanks."*

The unforgiving summer sun was beating down on us as we awkwardly stood in silence. I dared to sneak a peek at him once more when he removed the baseball cap and ran a hand through his hair.

Conner pressed the button on the crosswalk, and then he pulled the cap back on tightly. *"So, I was just going to go across the street and get a Gatorade or something."*

My stomach lurched in disappointment. That was my cue to get lost. Even at a young age, I knew when a boy wasn't interested in me. *"Oh, okay, I'll just walk back by myself."*

He grinned and said, *"You're not gonna come with me?"*

I didn't answer because I wasn't used to anyone wanting me around. I mean, my brothers obviously cared a great deal for me, but I was sure it got to be more of chore for them to be my babysitters.

"Come on, Shadow," he said.

"Shadow?"

"Yeah," he said and bumped my shoulder with his. "You're following me like you're my shadow."

I gnawed at my bottom lip as the butterflies in my stomach swirled and swirled. Turning around, I glanced back to where my brothers were still playing football and made my decision.

"Okay, I'll come with you," I said, then hesitated before stepping off the curb.

Conner smiled and asked, "What's wrong? You look like somebody stole your favorite toy or something."

Shifting from foot to foot, I said, "Nothing's wrong. It's just that I don't really know you. Like really know you, and my brothers might get mad at me for leaving, and—"

"My name is Conner Roberts. I'm thirteen years old. I just moved here from Pennsylvania a few weeks ago since my parents just got divorced, and this is where my mom's from originally. I have an older sister, Maggie, who is in high school. I like Batman . . . a lot. I don't have many friends yet and probably won't have many now thanks to your brothers."

He looked up to the vibrant blue sky as he thought about what he was going to say next.

"Oh," he said with a spark in his eyes when he looked my way again. "I met my shadow today, and I'm hoping that she'll be my friend and go with me to the store across the street."

I couldn't hide the smile that crept up on my face when he finished talking. I could only nod in agreement and follow him to the ends of the earth if he asked me. Instead, I settled on trailing behind him to the store, where he bought us each a Gatorade. Afterward, Conner walked me back to the park just in case my brothers were looking for me.

They were. And they weren't happy.

But Jonathan, always the mediator, stepped in and tried to defuse the tension by asking for a drink of my orange Gatorade. It worked. Simon walked away before attempting to embarrass me again.

"Don't worry about it, Katy," Jonathan said and handed me back the bottle. "Just don't wander off without telling at least one of us where you're going, okay?"

"They're just looking out for you," Conner said as we watched him walk away. "My sister can be a little overprotective too."

He smiled and asked, "So, same time tomorrow?"

"Sure."

I didn't think Conner would want to deal with Simon, so my hopes weren't very high that I'd ever see him again.

To my surprise, the next day came, and there he was waiting for me at the park.

And the day after that.

We were like two peas in a pod after that first day, and he became so much more to me than just a friend or confidant . . . he was everything.

CHAPTER EIGHT

S o that's how I ended up giving Katy the nickname Shadow."
Mimi smiles after Conner's detailed retelling of the first day we met, bringing the memory to the forefront of my mind in vivid Technicolor.

"I like that nickname for you, Katy," she says. "It kind of suits you perfectly, you know?"

"I liked it . . . I mean, I like it too. It's been so long since I've heard it, though; it's kind of strange hearing it now."

"How long has it been exactly?" Conner asks.

I pretend to take a little longer to calculate the years, months, weeks, and days in my head, as if I have no clue the actual amount of time that has gone by since we last saw and spoke to each other. Not like I've been pining away for him or anything. However, in front of him, the last thing I want to come off as is someone who's been doing exactly that for nine years and a month or two, give or take a few days. But who's counting . . . apparently me.

"A little over nine years, I think," I say, then quickly add, "I'm not sure exactly. Something like that."

"Wow, has it really been that long? It can't be," he says, then takes a sip of his beer. "I'm trying to remember the last time we saw each other."

Mimi's face goes slack. She's trying her hardest to keep a straight face and not break under the pressure. Thank God, for once she's not blabbing like the loose cannon that I know she can be.

"Oh, barmaid," a male patron calls from the other end of the bar. "Can we get a little service?"

Mimi curses under her breath and tells us she will be right back.

It's not that I'm embarrassed by the letter anymore . . . well, maybe a little bit. It's just that I don't want to rehash that part of my past with anyone, much less *with* Conner. And if I know Mimi well enough, she will have colorful commentary about the letter and how I still have it, and then who knows where we'll end up in that conversation.

I turn casually on my bar stool to face Conner, trying very hard not to be thrown off by the very handsome man he's become in the years that have stretched between us. His hazel eyes especially . . . they were always my favorite thing about him when we were young. It always felt like he could read my mind before the words would come tumbling out of my mouth. As he gazes upon me now, it's different.

Tugging some hair behind my ears and with a nervous smile, I say, "So."

"So? I can't believe it's really you."

"It's really me."

He searches my face for a few seconds, and the weight of his stare makes me want to look away, but I keep my attention trained on him. I watch as his expression shifts from simple curiosity to a beaming smile, as if he had found the missing piece to a puzzle.

"You grew up, Katy," he says finally. "You look . . . different."

"Like I said, it's been about nine years, so yeah, you could say that." My tone comes off as defensive.

He laughs. "I don't mean it in a bad way at all. I mean you look like—"

"Like what?"

"A woman," he says simply. "It's kind of gross."

My mouth drops open in shock until Conner laughs at my reaction. Then I start to laugh right alongside him. I playfully smack his upper arm. "Very funny."

"Well, it's true. I remember you being all gangly arms and legs and always fighting with your brothers." He takes another sip of his beer and then runs a hand through his hair. "Wait, that's not entirely true either. Just Simon . . . Jonathan was always pretty cool with me."

I roll my eyes at the mention of my brothers. "Simon hasn't changed much. He's a cop now, by the way."

"Really? That sounds like it would be perfect for him."

"Actually," I say, stopping to give a quick look around the bar and then the front door. "I'm surprised he's not even here yet. He's usually following me home or checking up on me at some point during the day *and* night."

"Wow! So he's still the same overprotective and overbearing big brother, huh?"

"Are we talking about Simon?" Mimi asks, propping her elbows on the bar. I nod and then she says, "He's still the same asshole you remember him to be, I bet."

"He was harmless," Conner says. "He was just looking after his baby sister."

I can't help the twinge of annoyance I feel at hearing him refer to me as the baby sister. It shouldn't, seeing as I'm older and know better. But the truth of it is that not only does Simon remind me of this fact regularly, but being around Conner again makes me feel that way too. Not in the sibling kind of way, but in that he's always going to see me as the gangly girl he grew up with.

"Yeah, but I'm not a baby anymore, Conner." Damn, there I go slipping into that defensive tone again.

But Conner doesn't detect it. Or if he does, he doesn't pay it any mind when he quietly says, "No, you're definitely not."

"Did you find out what he's been doing? Where he's been?" Mimi asks out of nowhere.

Conner smiles as I let Mimi know that I was working my way toward that but got sidetracked. "You might as well tell us at the same time, since she"—I point my finger at her—"won't quit until I tell her everything."

"Let's see," he says. "You already know I went away to college."

"Where did you go?" Mimi asks.

I already know the answer: UCLA, located on the other side of the country.

When I was sixteen, Los Angeles might as well have been Russia when my best friend and crush moved there. Back then, I was so hurt that I never bothered to get an e-mail or physical address from him to stay in touch. On the other hand, he obviously knew where I lived and not once sent a letter or called to see how I was doing. Then, within a year of Conner moving across the country, my parents were gone, and the life I knew was over . . . so he kind of became an afterthought. And as more and more time went by, he was just someone I used to know. Of course, I wondered what happened to him and where he was every so often. But that was always quickly followed by wondering why he never reached out to me . . . at least until now.

"I ended up staying there after completing my undergrad and going to medical school. I'm in my last year of residency, then I'll have another few years of a fellowship for sports medicine to complete before it's all said and done." Conner pauses and then thoughtfully looks at me. "It's actually because of Shadow here that I became as interested as I am in sports medicine."

"Me? How did that happen?"

Mimi groans. "Please warn me if we're about to launch into another hour-long discussion on sports. If we are, then tell me right now, because I have side work I could be doing to get out of here on time tonight."

Conner chuckles and shakes his head. "I take it you don't like sports, huh?"

"Pfft! Having to listen to Katy talk about football nonstop is more than meeting my daily quota on sports, thank you very much."

"Okay, we get the picture, Mimi," I say, half laughing, half annoyed because she interrupted him as he was about to tell us how I, of all people, inspired his life's calling. I pivot in my seat to give Conner my full attention again. "So, you were saying?"

"Oh right . . . sorry." He puts down his beer bottle and then turns in his stool to face me. "You don't remember, do you?"

"Remember what?" I ask at the same time Mimi does.

His mouth tips up in a teasing smile, and his hazel eyes twinkle with amusement while my mind starts racing, trying to remember exactly what he's talking about.

Conner leans forward and says, "Come here, I'll give you a hint."

Nervous at being this close to him, but very curious, I meet him halfway in the space between our bar stools. Obviously not satisfied with how close I am to him, he leans a little farther. In that handful of seconds, I close my eyes and inhale. I actually freeze the moment in my head and smell him like he's a fresh bouquet of roses or something. And in that instant of cataloging his scent, it brings to mind the brightness of the sun after a rain shower and how it makes everything more beautiful in the light of day.

A quick snap of Mimi's fingers brings me out of my break with sanity. I open my eyes; she rolls hers and then points like a crazy person at the back of Conner's head, which is poised by my ear. As if sharing a secret between old lovers, he speaks quietly, so only I can hear him.

"Knight in shining armor."

"Excuse me?"

As he leans back and smiles at me, he says a little louder now so Mimi can hear him, "That's your hint."

Conner watches as I search my memories. Many of them are of us as kids goofing around and playing in our neighborhood park, where we initially met. Later memories are of me not knowing what to say and feeling awkward around him; the whole time, Conner was oblivious to how I was developing a whopper of a crush on him.

"I'm disappointed, Shadow," he says finally. "I consider that moment to be one of my top five to this day."

The realization hits me then, and I smile shyly as the memory replays in my head. "I remember."

"For chrissakes, will one of you just say it already?" Mimi asks, exasperated.

"Shall I?" he asks me.

I shake my head and glance at Mimi, who looks as if she's about to lose her mind if one of us doesn't start telling the story.

"Hey, Bartender? Do you think you could spare us some of your time over here?"

This comes from the same guy as before at the other end of the bar, but this time his voice is infinitely more annoyed.

"You have got to be kidding me," Mimi grumbles under her breath. "The nerve of people . . . interrupting me to do my job. I'll be back, kids. Do not start without me."

As she hustles to the take the drink order, Conner starts to laugh. "She's pretty funny, Shadow. Where did you guys meet?"

"In high school during my sophomore year. We've been best friends ever since."

He half smiles, and if I'm not mistaken, I notice a bit of a grimace. Which really kind of bugs me. Because he had his chance to remain friends but didn't do anything about it.

"After my parents died, I was a bit of a mess. We all were . . . Simon and Jonathan included. I met Mimi almost right afterward. She has been nothing but loyal and honest and a true friend." I stop and realize that this conversation all of a sudden took a turn down a more serious route than I intended. So I try to make things light again. "Well, except for that time recently where she told my old best friend who I haven't seen in years that I would meet him tonight."

"You didn't want to meet me tonight?" he asks, his eyebrows pulling together in concern.

Placing my hand on his forearm gently, I say, "No, it's not like that at all, Conner. Of course I wanted to see you. Are you kidding? It's awesome seeing you again. But she kind of ambushed me and I was completely caught by surprise. It's a great surprise, I promise."

His smile unfurls slowly, like he's just now seeing me . . . *really* seeing me for the very first time in years. "It's really great to see you too, Shadow. And I'm so sorry I wasn't there for you when your parents died. I wanted to be, I really did, but—"

"Okay, I'm back. Get to talking," Mimi announces and puts a stop to Conner's explanation. "I had to buy that guy and his buddies a shot each to shut them up for a while."

"Well, I think I was twelve and—"

"You were thirteen and I was fifteen," Conner says adamantly.

"Okay, so I was thirteen and trying out for the soccer team at my junior high school." I then look to Conner, who is resting his chin in his hand while leaning against the bar. His eyes never leave my face as I start to get lost in the memory. "It was the third day of tryouts and there were maybe three or four of us that were vying for the forward position."

"She was really good," he says, looking at me.

"I'm sure," Mimi says, then shushes him so I can go on telling the story.

"Anyway, there was this one girl, Christina Cox, who was one year older than me who always played a little dirty."

"The little bitch," Mimi says under her breath.

"Since she was older too, she thought the position should automatically go to her. So when the coaches kept putting me in during scrimmage instead of her, she got really irritated. Finally, though, she got in the game."

"You should have seen this girl," Conner says to Mimi. "She was taller and broader than I was. She looked like she played for the Soviet Union men's hockey team and she was mean as hell."

Conner and I start to laugh until Mimi gets me to start the story again. "So there I was, making my way with the ball, passing to this one and that one, and right before I line up to make my shot, Christina comes out of nowhere and takes my legs out from under me."

"I told you she was a little bitch," Mimi says.

"It's not illegal to do that, but then she slammed her cleated foot down on my ankle when I was on the ground."

"I was watching from the sidelines," Conner says. "It was brutal. I have never in all my life wanted to hit a person of the opposite sex . . . except this one time. It took everything I had to just stand there and watch."

"Oh my God! What did the coaches say?" Mimi asks.

"They yelled at her and kicked her out of the tryouts, but it made no difference to me because I was in so much pain. Then . . ."

Conner sits up proudly and pretends to dust off his shoulders. "Then her knight in shining armor came to the rescue."

"The next thing I know, I'm being picked up off the ground by Conner," I say, stopping briefly to relish the memory. He whispered in my ear that he was going to pick me up and that I should put my arms around his neck. "He carried me off the field to the sidelines, and when I thought he was going to stop and put me down, he just kept right on carrying me home."

"It was like two miles, at least," he says.

"Shut up. It was more like two blocks," I say with a laugh. "Nobody was home, so Conner had to play doctor until my parents got there and took me to the emergency room."

"Oooh, playing doctor," Mimi says with a coy smile. "Smooth, Conner. Very smooth."

A sudden flush of embarrassment hits me, but Conner shakes it off with a laugh. Then he looks over to me and winks. "Her mom's the one who called me Katy's knight in shining armor and said I had a great bedside manner." He shrugs. "All I had done was get her some ice and make her keep her leg up on a pillow. I knew that it was probably a severe sprain, and the way she looked made me stay until her parents got there."

"How did I look?" I ask, genuinely curious. I glance over at Mimi, who's waiting with bated breath for Conner to explain too.

"Broken."

"Awww, Conner, that is the sweetest thing ever, and coming from me—trust me—that is saying a lot," Mimi says.

I, on the other hand, after hearing that one word, don't think of that day but the ones after that. Because that day changed everything between us. Or, changed *me* at least. I saw him in a completely different light; not as my friend, but as the boy I was slowly falling for more and more each day.

Mimi, who picks up on my silence as evidence that I'm having a moment, tries to bring the conversation back to life. "So, Conner, why are you in town?"

"I'm packing up my mom's stuff and getting the house ready to be put on the market since she's moving to New Hampshire to live with my sister and her family." Conner drinks the last of his beer and then puts the bottle on the bar. Mimi asks he if wants another, but he politely refuses. "No, thanks, I actually have to get going since I have a long day ahead of me tomorrow."

"How long are you in town for?" I ask.

"A couple of weeks or so. Maybe a little longer or a little less, depending on how quickly I get everything done. Luckily, I was able to take some time away from my residency to help out my mom, which was the least I could do considering all that she's done for me over the years."

"Well, it was really nice to meet you, Conner," Mimi says, putting out her hand for him to shake. "I really do have some side work to get done if I want to get out of here tonight. Katy, I'll see you at home."

She darts away as Conner stands up and takes a few bills out of his wallet to leave on the bar. As he tucks it back into his pocket, he asks, "What are you doing tomorrow?"

"Me?"

"Yeah, you."

"Um, nothing." Then I realize I usually play beach volleyball mini tournaments with Dylan one Saturday a month. And tomorrow is *that* Saturday. "Wait, I have a volleyball game on the beach tomorrow."

"Can you skip it?" he asks.

Can I? *Would* I skip it is more the question to ask myself. I've never missed a Saturday volleyball tournament before. But it's not like it's the Olympics or anything, so it wouldn't be a big deal, right? Then I think Conner is only visiting for a little while, and Dylan would understand if I wanted to spend time with an old friend. So yes, I'm sure it wouldn't be a big deal.

"Yes."

He puts his hand out to help me up from my bar stool and then bends down to grab my messenger bag for me. As I pull it over my head, I can feel Conner staring at me. Not in a creepy way, but in the curious, trying-to-figure-me-out kind of way again.

"Why do you keep looking at me like that?" I ask, half laughing, half serious. "You're giving me the heebie-jeebies."

He shakes his head and chuckles through a sigh. "It's nothing. I'm just having a hard time wrapping my head around the fact that you're a grown-up."

"Ditto."

The silence stretches between us for a few beats until he says, "Okay, so tomorrow. Can you meet me at my mom's house? Say around eleven? And don't worry, I won't make you do you any heavy lifting."

"Sure, sounds good."

The time has come when we're supposed to say good night to each other, but what is the protocol? As kids, we'd just bump fists or give each other a high five. But now it's weird. Do we kiss on the cheek and hug again? I'm not sure what to do, and by the look on Conner's face, neither is he. Glad to know that I'm not the only one perplexed by this situation.

Finally, Conner takes a step toward me, and I think it's to give me a hug good-bye, so I step in a little closer too. Our signals are all kinds of crossed, because he leans forward as my arms wrap around his neck for a friendly hug. My face is tilted up when he attempts to kiss me on the cheek, only to end up kissing me on the corner of my mouth because I didn't move my face in time.

We're both laughing at how awkward that was. But I can't lie to myself about not enjoying the tiniest feel of his lips on mine finally, for the briefest of seconds and if only the one time.

"Sorry, I didn't mean to do that."

"It's okay. We might need to work on that a little," I joke.

Conner raises an eyebrow. "So, tomorrow? Eleven?"

"See you there."

Then he goes to leave, turning around one final time when he reaches the door to wave good-bye. I stand there frozen in the same spot where he left me at the bar, staring at the door for a few seconds after he's gone. As if I'm waiting for something else to happen. What that something is, I don't know. And it isn't until I hear a bottle shatter on the hardwood floor somewhere in the distance that the spell is broken.

My attention goes to Mimi behind the bar, and I see that she's busy, so I simply shout out a quick good night to her. I drive home consumed by the idea of spending the day with Conner. I do manage to snap out of my thoughts of him long enough to finalize the article I had been working on and email it over to Dylan for approval. When I receive his return email ten minutes later saying that everything looks great, my mind goes right back to Conner. The thought of him brings a smile to my face, and it stays there as I get under the covers to sleep.

Just the two of us again.

Like two peas in a pod.

CHAPTER NINE

I'm awakened by the best smell ever: freshly brewed coffee. I'm shocked and delighted, since Mimi is not one to brew a pot of coffee ever. There must be a special reason or it's the end of the world. Whichever it is, it gets my eyes open after sleeping in longer than usual on a Saturday.

The bright Florida sun peeks through the blinds on the window over my bed, and it takes me a second or two to adjust to it. Rubbing my eyes with the heels of my hands, I kick my feet out of the bed and into my slippers. With a quick stretch, I'm off to have my morning cup of joe.

"Well, well, well," Mimi says. "If it isn't Sleeping Beauty."

"Good morning to you too."

Opening the cabinet that has our huge collection of coffee mugs, I grab one and put it under the coffee machine, then press the lever down so that it will dispense a full cup of morning goodness. Behind me, I feel Mimi's impatient stare, followed by her foot tapping on the floor.

When I turn around, she has her hands on her hips.

"What?" I ask. "Why are you looking at me like you're going to kill me?"

"Seriously?"

"Yeah, seriously. What did I do?"

"Um, hello! Conner. Last night. Bar. Tension. The sexual kind. And no, I'm so not wrong on this one."

I almost choke on my coffee. Once I clear my throat, I stare at her in amazement. "What the hell are you talking about? Tension, the sexual kind? There was no sexual tension. He's just an old friend."

"Thank God you have me in your life," she says, looking up at the ceiling.

I have to laugh. "What does that mean?"

She comes over to where I'm standing and takes the mug out of my hands. As if placing a newborn baby down for a nap, she ever so gently puts it down on the counter between us. Then she takes both my hands in hers and with the most serious face I've ever seen on her, proceeds to tell me whatever is on her mind.

"Sweetie," she says in a sugary voice. "That man—and girl, he is *soooo* fine, I don't blame you one bit for being hung up on him—he's attracted to you. He wants to get into your pants. He wants to know if the carpet matches the drapes. He wants to make you howl at the moon like a dog from behind. He wants to—"

"Are you high?!" I step away from her. Yanking my hands from her increasing death grip, I add, "I mean, seriously, did you take, like, an Ambien or something and mix it with a Red Bull? Because you are freaking nuts!"

"I'm just trying to help you out."

"With what, exactly?"

"With seeing the signs." Mimi climbs onto the counter and crosses her legs with all the flourish of a flamenco dancer. "Listen, he is not the same guy you knew. He's older, wiser, definitely hotter, and I'll bet you a million dollars that he's one hundred percent kicking himself for not having taken your V card when he had the chance."

"He is not."

"Yes he is."

"No, he's not, Mimi."

"Oh yes he is, Katy."

I sigh and lean against the counter. "Okay, I give. What makes you think all of this?"

"The way he whispered that little hint in your ear. Or the way he winked at you all playful and was totally flirting with you." She puts both her hands underneath her chin and then blinks hers eyes in quick succession. "Oh! And the way he noticed that you definitely aren't a little girl anymore."

I was there when all of this happened. Either I'm the world's biggest idiot or I'm completely clueless, because not once last night did I get the impression that Conner was into me. Did he mention how I'm all grown up a couple of times? Sure, but that doesn't translate into being interested in me.

"Nope, I don't see it, Mimi." I reach for my coffee mug again. Holding it at my lips before taking a sip, I say, "I'll prove you wrong when I see him today."

"Hold the fucking phone! What did you just say?"

"I said, I'm going to see him today. And I'll prove you wrong."

"Wait a second. Back up to when he asked you out. Because I missed that part of the conversation," she says.

I roll my eyes. "There's really nothing to tell. He asked me to come over to his mom's house today. He's helping to pack up all of her things since she moved to his sister's in New Hampshire. That's it. No funny business."

She stays quiet for a few seconds. Then she smiles wide. "I'm not going to say another word about it. But promise me one thing, okay?"

"Fine, what?"

"You'll tell me when it's okay to say I told you so. Because as sure as the day is long, I will be saying I told you so sooner than later."

Right then, the doorbell rings, and we both look at each other in confusion. That is, until I glance at the clock on the microwave over Mimi's shoulder and it registers.

Dylan.

Oh God, I am the worst friend in the universe.

Mimi hops off the counter to answer it. When she opens the door, she announces, "It's one of your men, Katy."

Inwardly, I groan, because for the millionth time I'm going to have to explain to her that: (A) Dylan is not one of my men, (B) I have no other man to have a list going all of a sudden, and finally, (C) Dylan is a friend, just like Conner.

Dylan is so good-natured about Mimi's ribbing. He's been in on it for as long as I can remember, so it doesn't even faze him.

"Mornin' ladies."

Dylan strolls into our apartment as he pushes his sunglasses up onto his head. He's dressed to play beach volleyball. In one hand he's spinning his keys and in the other is a to-go cup of Starbucks coffee. He takes a couple more steps toward me in the kitchen and looks over my pajamas and bedhead.

"Why aren't you ready?" Dylan asks.

"Humph, and you say he's not one of your men." Mimi says this as she turns on her heel and walks down the hallway to her bedroom. Then she shouts suddenly, "Make it work!"

He jerks his thumb over his shoulder and says with a chuckle, "What does she mean *one* of your men?"

I smile. "Forget about her. She's just being crazy as usual. Listen, Dylan, when I turned in the article last night I meant to tell you that I needed to cancel our plans today."

His bright green eyes scan me from head to toe in one fell swoop. I immediately regret not putting on my robe after I got out of bed, since I'm sure my boobs are on full display through my thin white tank top, and I have on barely there shorts. I'm practically naked, so I immediately cross my arms to cover my chest. Granted, he's seen me in a bikini before, but there is something more intimate about bedclothes and undergarments. Especially when it's a man who's taking it all in.

"What's wrong? Are you sick?" I catch his gaze quickly going from my now covered chest to my face. "Do you need me to run out and get you some medicine or something?"

Seeing him all anxious to please me—as a friend, of course—and even if it is simply to get me medicine for an ailment that doesn't exist, makes me feel incredibly guilty that I'm cancelling our plans. But when I got home last night, I had to give my article a quick once-over. Then I pressed Send and that was it. Not to mention that the idea of spending the day with Conner was kind of at the forefront of my mind, blocking out any and all other thoughts before falling asleep.

"No, I'm totally fine." I hesitate before telling him the rest for some reason. "I'm spending the day with an old friend who is in town for just a couple of weeks."

He relaxes a little, the tension visibly leaving his face, and he smiles brightly at me. "Do I know her?"

"Her?"

"Yeah, your friend that you're spending the day with. Do I know her?"

Of course he would assume he might know my friend since we've been friends for so long, and I have such a very small circle of friends. Actually, I really only have Mimi and Dylan . . . and I guess my brothers. Who don't count since, well, they're family.

Nervously, I take a chunk of my hair and start to tie it in a loose knot before undoing it, then immediately do it all over again. "Um, no. And it's not a she. It's a he."

"Oh."

There's a noticeable shift in the room with his one-syllable answer.

Unsure of what to do next, I try to think of something to say to fix this. But I struggle to find the right words. "Listen, Dylan, I—"

"Yup, sounds about right," Mimi says under her breath as she storms back and grabs her coffee mug. "Forgot my coffee."

"Shut up, Mimi." Turning my attention back to Dylan, I say, "Ignore her."

"It's fine, Katy. I can get someone else to sub for you. Go ahead and have a great time catching up with . . ." He makes a face like he's trying to remember something.

"With Conner," I say.

"Right. With Conner."

I could swear he says Conner's name as if he has a wad of peanut butter on the roof of his mouth and can't quite get his tongue to let the word roll off of it. But that's probably because I've put him out this morning by driving out of his way to pick me up. And in reminding myself of this fact, I start all over again with the self-induced and well-deserved guilt trip.

"I'm really sorry, Dylan. I really should have told you last night or at least called you this morning."

Dylan's demeanor changes and he laughs off my screwup like it's nothing. "It's not a big deal, Katy. Go and have a great day with your friend. We'll catch up later."

I let go of the chunk of hair I've been twirling and knotting. "Okay, so I'll see you in the office on Monday?"

He's already walking to the front door. It's not a huge apartment, but it seems like for every step he takes, I have to take at least four to keep up with him.

He still hasn't answered me, so when I catch up to him and hold the door open, I ask again, "Dylan, I'll see you Monday, right?"

Reaching out, my hand latches on to his forearm before he walks past me. His skin feels both soft and warm under my touch. When we look down at the same time at the point of contact, I quickly snatch back my hand. And if I'm not crazy, it makes this moment feel more uncomfortable than it already was.

"Yeah, sure. Of course. I'll see you Monday." He tells me this while backing farther away and through the door I'm still holding open for him.

And then he's gone. Practically racing down the walkway to his car, barely sparing me a second glance and no wave good-bye.

"I'm such a shit," I say to myself quietly.

Closing the door, I lean my forehead against it and sigh out loud. Then a thought occurs to me, and I smile to myself. I'll take Dylan out to lunch on Monday when we're back at the office, my treat, to his favorite place to make it up to him.

Standing up straight, I instantly feel better about the whole thing and put it right out of my head. But then another thought pops in, this one is infinitely trickier, at least according to Mimi . . . Conner. I look over my shoulder at the clock on the microwave again and see that I have a couple of hours to (1) find an outfit to wear, and (2) get myself to his mom's house by eleven o'clock. To accomplish this, I'm going to have to bite the bullet and ask for advice from the one person who has way better fashion sense than anyone else I know.

With a reluctant groan, I shout out her name.

I hear her happy little jaunt into the living room before I see her and try to put on a straight face. "I need your help."

"With juggling your men? Girl, you are on your own with that hot mess."

"No, and would you cut that out already," I tell her. "I need your help with finding something to wear to see Conner."

Her eyes go wide. Her mouth drops open a little. And then finally, she makes a strange strangled sound.

"Mimi, are you okay?"

She comes out of her stupor, then runs off down the hallway, yelling out to me, "I thought you'd never ask."

CHAPTER TEN

W hen I arrive at Conner's mom's house, I'm already regretting my decision to let Mimi dress me.

She chose a pair of very short shorts in a royal blue that if I were a year or two older, I would not be able to get away with wearing. Above them is a black linen swing tank top that makes me feel more uneasy than the shorts, believe it or not, since it forces me to wear a racerback bra that puts my cleavage uncomfortably on display. This paired with black flip-flops that have a simple decorative flower on them, as Mimi says, for effect. I drew the line at jewelry, because if there is one thing I can't stand to be bothered with, it is an accessory, or two, or three. The worst part is that she didn't let me bring one hair tie to pull my hair up, which is my natural inclination within minutes of leaving my house and going anywhere. I officially feel more self-conscious than ever about my appearance.

But when I turn my attention to his childhood home, I'm calmed. The dozen or so amaranth plants I had helped Conner and his mom plant years ago are in full bloom. Their deep wine-red leaves are spilling over and look beautiful against the plain, cream-colored stucco of the ranch house. I park my car behind what I assume must be his rental during his visit and step out into the blazing midday sun.

As I walk the few steps to the front door, my heart feels like it's pounding so hard that it might jump right out of my chest. So I take a few breaths before ringing the doorbell. When it's not answered, I press the button again, only to hear Conner's voice come from the backyard.

"Katy, come around, I'm back here."

I walk the perimeter of the house and reach the backyard gate, opening it and laughing at the same time. The latch still gets stuck and won't open if you don't jimmy it just so. The stepping stones from the back gate to the patio that surrounds the pool are exactly the same, bringing to mind the countless times I would hop on them from one foot to the other. The older I got, the less difficult it became, until I was able to just walk them like everyone else.

I'm looking down at the steps when I hear him again. "There you are. Right on time."

This is bad. So bad.

Because Conner is standing right at the edge of the pool with just his swim trunks on, holding an aluminum pole that is submerged in the water, obviously cleaning it.

I still haven't said a word. And I'm afraid that I must look ridiculous, staring openmouthed at an adult-sized Conner in all his male glory . . . shirtless, to top it off. Conner was fit when we were younger and ran track here and there, but he wasn't super athletic or really into working out. But this Conner . . . this one is way different.

As he moves the brush against the walls of the pool, his arms flex again and again, showcasing perfectly developed muscles in his biceps and forearms. His chest has a smattering of hair that thins out down his flat stomach and disappears to . . .

Stop and get a grip, Katy! I yell in my head to snap out of the leering I'm in the middle of doing. Then I remind myself, *he's your friend.*

"Shadow?" Conner asks. "Are you okay?"

"Yeah, I'm fine," I choke out. I walk a little farther until I'm standing next to him, trying my hardest to keep from staring. "You should have let me know to bring my suit. It could have been like old times."

"Like old times, huh?" He laughs.

"Yeah, a little swim and some barbecue. Maybe another day."

"There won't be many chances left after this weekend. And once I'm gone, the house will be empty and officially on the market."

Does that mean I should run home and get my swimsuit? Wait, what am I thinking? I can't go swimming with grown-up Conner. It's not like we can play Marco Polo at our age or anything like that. It would be more awkward than it already is, at least for me. So, no, definitely not going home to get my bikini.

"Katy?"

"Yeah, here, sorry." I chuckle. Fanning myself, because I'm overheating from being underneath the sun and being around him, I go to sit on one of the chairs underneath the awning over the patio. "It's really hot, right?"

"It feels great," he says. "I'll be done in a minute. Help yourself to something to drink. There's a cooler right behind you."

I turn in my seat and, sure enough, there's a bright green Igloo cooler behind me. I reach over and pop it open, finding a few Corona bottles. They look absolutely delicious and like the perfect remedy to cool off. Tied with an old shoestring on one of the handles of the cooler is a bottle opener. I'm in the middle of using it when I hear a big splash.

Oh no. Should I turn around? If I do, then I'll have to watch Conner get out of the pool soaking wet, and I'm sure he looks even better that way. The mere thought of water sluicing down his body has me in a panic. I curse myself as I search for my sunglasses, which I was sure I brought with me, then realize that I left them *and* my purse in my car. Dammit.

Oh well, here goes nothing. Poker face, don't fail me now.

Turning around again, I am just in time to catch Conner hoisting himself ever so slowly out of the deep end of the pool. His back is to me, so I get to see his sinewy muscles tighten and stretch as they work together to get this fine piece of man out of the pool safely. It's like watching an ad for Cool Water Davidoff come to life right before my eyes.

He walks toward me, not even stopping when he yanks a towel off a chaise longue. He doesn't dry himself; instead, he wraps it around his waist and then pulls up a chair alongside me with a big smile.

"That felt amazing! I really needed that after working on the pool for the past couple of hours."

"I'm sure." I look everywhere but at him. The ground, the sky, the pool, the fence. Then I say, "It's the perfect kind of day to take a dip."

"Um, Shadow," he says quietly. I turn to look at him head-on. "If you want, you can take a dip."

My laugh sounds almost maniacal. "Me? A dip? Are you kidding? I already told you, I don't have my bikini with me. I'd have to go in my bra and underwear."

"I promise I'll close my eyes and won't peek."

Then he winks. Again. For the second time in as many days.

I stand up so fast that I almost knock the chair backward. "I have to go to the bathroom bad."

He chuckles and points toward the house. "Go ahead. You know where it is."

I walk as calmly as I can until I'm in the house and out of his view. Then I'm sprinting across to the other side of his house to go out the front door and to my car. I lean across the console to grab my purse and start fishing around for my cell phone to text Mimi for advice. And undoubtedly to have her tell me "I told you so."

Pressing the button to bring the phone to life, I see a text from Dylan.

Did you think you could get away without a question today? Here you go, Superstar . . . Who was the first person in the NFL to rush for over 1000 yards?

I smile, feeling relief at receiving his text and that he thought about me. I text back quickly:

Beattie Feathers

And just like that, I'm myself again. That's all I needed: a text from Dylan to put me back on track.

I see the little dots stringing together, so I know he's already texting me back. Then it flashes on my screen.

I have no words. You are a goddess.

Another string of dots and then:

Of football knowledge.

"Katy?"

"Oh my God! You scared me to death!"

It's true. Conner scared the living daylights out of me, so much that my phone fell out of my grasp and onto the ground. Thank the Lord I have a super-duper protector on it; if not, the screen would have shattered into a million pieces.

He's thankfully found some clothes by way of an old, beat-up baby blue T-shirt to cover up all that . . . all that stuff.

With a confused look on his face, he asks, "What are you doing out here? I thought you were going to the bathroom?"

"Sorry, I was, but then remembered I needed to send Dylan a message."

I don't know why I say this to him. It's a complete and utter bald-faced lie.

"Who's Dylan?"

"My boss at the newspaper." I'm slightly more calm and comfortable with the lie *and* the fact that he's dressed. "Just wanted to make sure he looked over my article before it was published this morning. And get any notes or suggestions on it and stuff."

I hear myself rambling on, and it doesn't even sound like me, like the Katy I am. I'm a strong, independent woman who doesn't sweat the small stuff. I have a job that requires me to be at the top of my game since it's a man's world . . . and yet, here I am, acting like a bumbling idiot because Conner had his shirt off.

Katy, get yourself together!

Once I repeat that phrase one more time in my head, the tension and nervous knot in my stomach releases.

"Listen, Katy, if you have work that you need to do, we can reschedule for another day."

I can tell he means it by the way his eyes soften around the edges, looking generally concerned for me.

"I'm fine. But don't you have to get some stuff packed? Won't I be in the way?"

He comes over to me and puts his arm around my shoulder, then proceeds to guide us toward the house, walking side by side with me. The faintest tremble of nerves comes back at the feel of him so close to me, almost holding me, but I squash it as quickly as it surfaces. I cannot let him see me as anything but cool, calm, and collected. I breathe in from my nose and out from my mouth. So fast and quiet that he doesn't even notice it.

When we reach the front door, he lets me go and holds it open for me.

And as I brush past him, he faintly says, "Shadow, you were never in the way."

CHAPTER ELEVEN

The rest of the day sped by.

Because as it turns out, Conner didn't do anything other than pack up stuff the remainder of the afternoon I was at his house. All I did, since he would not let me help him, was sit and watch. But it allowed us the time to really catch up with each other.

He told me about living in California. About his life, his friends, his dog—a Labrador retriever named Alfred who is being cared for by one his friends while he's away—his career, and finally, his personal life.

Broaching the subject of girlfriends and dating with Conner wasn't as difficult as I thought it would be. Because he was semi-distracted by all the boxes and the sheer magnitude of the task ahead of him, when he spoke about his past relationships, he was open and honest and left me feeling as if I was getting a glimpse at the real Conner, the one that I used to know and still wanted to know as a friend today.

He definitely isn't a ladies' man or anything like that. I mean, he has had women in his past. I would have to be dense not to think that. But it wasn't a bevy of them. However, there was one woman he spoke of fondly, almost reverently.

Her name is Abby, and when they met a few years ago, she was also in the midst of her residency. Conner said she had been part of his study group and they'd clicked immediately. They were together for over a year, and the breakup had been amicable because they had both realized that juggling a serious relationship while trying to complete their residencies was far too much pressure. Not to mention the little amount of free time they had to devote to each other.

"It kind of sucked to end it. I cared a lot about her," he said. "Actually, now that I think of it, she kind of reminded me of you."

This caught me totally off guard. "Why is that?"

"Well, for one thing, she is a rabid San Diego Chargers fan."

"There's no accounting for taste," I said with a look of fake contempt. "Everyone knows I'm a rabid Dolphins fan. Even though they break my heart every season."

"You know what I mean," he said, laughing at my reaction. "Anyway, her personality reminded me of you. She's not afraid to push or challenge herself to do new things. You know, it's not that easy for women in the sports medicine field. And she never lets that fact get her down. She always squares her shoulders and moves straight ahead."

"Sounds like I'd really like her."

I meant it. I probably would. But the tiniest twinge of jealousy wraps itself around my heart and squeezes it tight. The me of years past always wondered what it would have been like to be one of Conner's girlfriends. Today, as he told me about a couple of them, I not only wondered, but actually put myself in their shoes. When he left the room a few times, I daydreamed of how it would be if we were together like that. Would he kiss me hello as soon as he walked in the door after a long day? Would he snuggle and hold me in his arms at night and keep me close? Would he do little things to remind me how much he loved me?

As soon as I felt my imagination start to go over the deep end, I immediately stopped myself. Because what's the point? One, he's only here for a couple of weeks. Two, he has his life in California and I have mine here in Florida. Three, am I supposed to ask him to throw me a bone at least once, since he owes me after all these years? And finally, it's Conner . . . there is no way it can happen. Even if Mimi is even the slightest bit right in her assumption that he was maybe being a little flirtatious last night, and a bit today, that doesn't mean a thing. At the end of the day, he doesn't see me as anything other than the friend I was to him. Which is fine . . . *I'm* fine. *He's* fine. We're *all* fine.

As I was leaving his mom's house, he was quick to tell me that the next day would be difficult to get together. To be honest, I was a little surprised that he was already planning to see me again so soon. His day would be chock-full of visits from repairmen getting the house ready for the inspection scheduled for the end of the week. But he said that he'd call or text me at some point to make plans.

Instead of going home, I drive straight to Jonathan's townhouse on the beach. I don't even know why. In the past, whenever I've popped in to see Jonathan, it's usually because I had a huge looming deadline or a lot on my plate at work and I needed to unwind. He always ends up propping me in the lounger on his balcony that overlooks the ocean and giving me a blanket to wrap myself in, leaving me alone to relax. I'll sit and stare out at the horizon and watch the sun barely kiss the water as it slowly disappears for the day. By then, my head is clear and more focused and the stress that had gotten me into such a frazzled state is gone.

Until the next time . . . like today.

It's a Saturday, so he might not be home. Or maybe he has company and doesn't want his little sister around to cramp his style. I doubt it, but I text him anyway at a stoplight to see if the coast is clear, and he gives me the okay to head over.

Jonathan takes one look at me and holds the door open wide. I walk past him and head straight to the balcony. Luckily, I'm just in time to catch the sun being swallowed up whole by the ocean until there are only the stars in the night sky and the sounds of the waves crashing onto the shore.

A blanket is carefully placed around my shoulders, and usually I'd let Jonathan just walk away and leave me alone for a bit. But tonight, what I need most is his company.

"You don't have to leave," I say, not turning around but feeling his presence still. "Hang out with me for a bit."

He pulls up a chair, and then he's sitting and staring at the same view. "It's really beautiful, isn't it?"

"Yeah, it's amazing."

I pull the blanket tighter around me and over my shoulders, allowing only my eyes to peek up and over the rim to see the beauty play out before me.

"Is everything all right, Katy?"

"Yeah, I think so."

"You think so?" he asks.

"It was just a weird day. Actually, it's been a weird couple of days."

Jonathan doesn't say a thing for a few beats. Then he turns his chair a fraction to his left so it's facing me. He leans forward and rests his elbows on his knees. "Do you want to talk about it?"

"Only if you promise not to tell Simon."

He smiles and his eyes warm instantly at my request. "You know you don't ever have to make me promise that."

After a long pause and then a sigh, I ask him, "Do you remember Conner?"

It takes him a few seconds, but then the name finally registers.

"Wow, that's a name I haven't heard in a long time. Whatever happened to him?"

"He's in town for a couple of weeks and looked me up. I just came from his house before I got here to see you."

Jonathan takes this information in and doesn't say a word.

"And?" he asks after a few more beats of silence.

"And what?"

He waves his hand up and down my body. "Why does seeing Conner again have you like this? I thought you guys were best friends back in the day."

With a tight smile, I say, "I know, but that was forever ago. Plus . . . things got kind of weird between us before he went away to college."

"Weird how?"

"And we didn't stay in touch all these years." I stop to take a quick breath, because I can feel myself getting more worked up with every passing second. "Who does that? I mean, someone that you spend almost every single day of your childhood and adolescence with and then poof! Nothing, not one word for nine years! And I'm supposed to not ask about it because then it would be even weirder between us."

"Weird *how*, Katy?"

I ignore Jonathan again and keep right on going. "Then last night I think we're having a normal conversation. But Mimi thought he was totally flirting with me and wants to get in my pants, which is crazy . . . because that would be super weird. Like weird on another level of weird that they haven't even invented yet. I think—"

"Whoa! Stop for a second and take a breath!"

Jonathan lets me be quiet long enough to compose myself and, more importantly, get my breathing back to normal. If I keep on going—which I probably could—I'll start to hyperventilate. And for what? I don't even know why, if I'm being honest with myself. Is it simply because I want to know why Conner waited so long to get in touch with me? Or maybe I need for him to explain to me how he could just leave me behind if I meant so much to him and apparently had such a big impact on his career choice?

"Do you think you can talk calmly about it now?"

"I don't know. Give me another minute."

We sit in silence while I try to string together all my thoughts so that they are semi-coherent. That's when I realize I told my own brother about someone possibly wanting to have sex with me. If there is one subject never to be broached with your brother, it's your sex life.

Closing my eyes and covering them with my hands for good measure, I ask. "Did I just tell you that Conner wants to get in my pants? I did, didn't I?"

Jonathan laughs uneasily. "Yup, you definitely did. We'll get back to that momentarily."

"Can we pretend I didn't? Because I'd really rather not get into that right now again. It's bad enough that I have Mimi telling me almost every day for the past few years that Dylan wants to get into my pants and now Conner? It's driving me crazy all on its own."

"Dylan? How did he get into this mess?"

With a sigh, I rub my face with my hands and then run them through my hair in frustration. "Never mind. Forget I brought him and the whole pants thing up."

"Do you want my advice or not?"

"I'm not so sure anymore."

He chuckles like he's enjoying my misery. "Look, it's easy. Conner always seemed like a good guy to me—"

"He still is, Jonathan. That's what makes me more confused."

"Confused how, though? It should be nothing but easy. Guys aren't very hard to figure out."

I raise an eyebrow at that comment. "Oh really? I beg to differ."

"Katy, let me break it down for you so you can understand."

I reach out to smack him on his arm, but he catches my hand in midair while laughing. "Seriously, it's not that hard. Guys are either into you or they're not. They either are attracted to you in that . . . *way*. Or they're not."

"No? Really? Gosh, thanks for that explanation. You magically solved my dilemma."

He ignores my sarcasm. "Let me ask you this, which is probably more important and probably what has you in such a tizzy—"

"Do grown men really use the word 'tizzy'?"

"Would you be interested in Conner if it turned out he was interested in you?"

My knee-jerk reaction is already at the tip of my tongue with a big fat sign that says YES. But is that what I would truly want? If you asked the sixteen-year-old version of me, she'd bow down to the gods and not even question herself. But now, it's not that cut-and-dried. Because if I jumped into bed with him at the first opportunity, no matter how many years have gone by and no matter how much I tell myself that it's not a big deal, my heart will be involved. How could it not be where Conner's concerned?

"I don't know." Tugging some hair behind my ears, I say, "What do you think?"

"Katy, don't ask me a stupid question, because you're only going to get a stupid answer."

"I know, I know, I'm deflecting."

"Look," he says. "If it's right, you'll know. If not, then move on. But no matter what, don't let anyone or anything pressure you to do anything you don't want to do."

My smile is faint, but it's genuine, because as vague as his advice is, it makes me feel better. "Thanks, Jonathan."

"Now what about Dylan?"

That's my cue to stand up and throw aside the blanket. "Nothing, forget I ever mentioned him."

"Katy, he may be your friend, but don't forget, he's also your boss."

He says this as I'm walking through the sliding doors to leave. "I know. I'm not stupid. Plus, he's too good of a friend to me to consider that. I swear, if I lost my friendship with Dylan, I'd be a lot worse than what you just witnessed."

And with that sound, personal advice, I say good-bye and go home to bed.

CHAPTER TWELVE

M onday, and I'm in full swing already at six o'clock in the morning, driving to the newsroom.

I spent my Sunday on the couch with the NFL's opening week games on in the background while I did some research on the Barracudas' next opponent. I always do a smaller piece on the upcoming week's game and publish it on the newspaper's website on Wednesday afternoons. A rough first draft is completed by Monday. Then Tuesday I'll follow up on stats and numbers and confirm my sources. Then, on Wednesday morning, everything is crosschecked one more time . . . and then again for safe measure. All that's left is to type up my final draft and review it a couple of more times before turning it in. This leaves Thursday open to attend the final practice before the Barracudas play on Friday night. And then my schedule starts all over again.

This is how I spend most of my fall at the newspaper. It's my busy time . . . and I love it. Then it's on to soccer and cross-country, followed by baseball.

But I look forward to the football season like a kid on Christmas morning. Because as much as there is a feeling of magic and pure Americana attached to baseball, it doesn't make me feel the emotions that football does, from heartbreak to pure bliss.

Even though I get to work a little earlier than usual, the office is already at top gear. I walk straight to Dylan's office instead of my desk to invite him out to lunch today at his favorite spot. And I won't take no for an answer.

Phoebe, his assistant from hell, isn't at her command center yet, so I can just walk in.

I hear him on the phone before I see him, so I stay out of sight until he's done. Trying not to listen, I overhear him say "Rachel" followed by him laughing. Then he's saying something about maybe getting together this weekend to play some volleyball again if she's up to it.

Rachel? Rachel from accounting upstairs? That's who subbed for me this weekend?

Ugh.

Rachel Aguirre has been trying for as long as I've been working at the newspaper to get her hooks into Dylan. She's a tall, leggy blonde with boobs for days. And she's not shy about showing them off either. She's been a bit pushy and, for lack of a better word, bitchy when I've had to deal with her in the past. Which isn't often, but every couple of months or so she comes strolling downstairs to my desk to question me about my expense report and the validity of a certain receipt or something . . . I don't know, because for the most part, I, like every red-blooded male in the office, am staring at her chest. It would be impossible not to since she's always wearing a low-cut blouse to showcase it. Then she'll lean over the desk, which I swear she's doing on purpose to make sure you get a good, long look at the goods. Which I do look at, of course I do. I mean, who could blame me? They're spectacular. And if Dylan is anywhere in the vicinity, she perks up, adjusting her cleavage and smiling like the devil in disguise to get his attention.

Well, looks like she got it finally. I could have sworn that he's told me more than a couple of times that he would never, ever, be interested in her. But I guess things change.

"Katy, is that you hovering outside my door?"

I put on a straight face and peek my head around the frame. "Hey, yeah, it's me."

Glancing at his wristwatch, he says, "You're here early."

"I wanted to get a head start today. But I needed to see you first before you made any plans."

"Plans? Plans for what?" He looks up, his green eyes bright and cheery through his black-rimmed eyeglasses.

"You, me, lunch. And I won't take no for an answer."

He leans back in his chair and goes for the knot in his tie. As he begins to loosen it, he says, "You don't have to do that."

"I want to," I tell him. "Plus, we haven't been to your favorite lunch spot in a while. Figure we're due."

Dylan doesn't say anything, so I naturally start to adjust and readjust my messenger bag nervously. "Come on." I break the silence. "Just say yes and meet me downstairs at noon, okay?"

Finally, the faintest trace of a smile shows through on his face. It's small, but I'll take it. "Okay, sure, I'll meet you downstairs at noon."

"Great! See you then."

I walk out of his office feeling uneasy, even though the fakest smile is plastered across my face. I get the sense that Dylan's just saying yes to lunch to appease me and that he really doesn't want to go. But why? He's never been one to be phony. So today, after seven or eight years of knowing each other, why would he start acting that way out of the blue? Or maybe he . . .

No. No way.

I have to stop letting Mimi's stupid idea seep into my thoughts. Because that would go against everything our friendship has been based upon. We're always professional when we have to be and, other times, great friends who give each other advice when needed. And that's it. Nothing more, nothing less.

When I reach my desk, I plop down in my seat, still confused. Why would Dylan be put off by my invitation? Wait, was he put off? No, that can't be right. I'm just imagining things. He was probably in the middle of something and I caught him at a bad time. He had just been on the phone with Rachel.

Is that what's bugging me? The idea of Rachel and Dylan together? I have to laugh, because why would that bother me? I don't like her, but as his friend, I want *him* to be happy. And if she makes him happy, then so be it. As his friend, I'll support him in whatever he decides.

"They're not picking out china patterns yet or anything, so just stop it already." I say this to myself quietly and get to work so that lunch will come sooner than later.

After placing our order at the counter, Dylan and I look for an open table, which is a little difficult since Gilbert's is always bursting at the seams with customers at lunchtime.

"Oh, there's one." I point at a two-seat high-top table in the far corner by the window.

We weave through the other tables until reaching ours. Dylan pulls my seat out for me, and I sit down, placing my phone on the table. While I'm lifting my messenger bag strap over my head, he sits across from me and places our assigned number for our order on the table in between us.

"Next time, I'm paying," he says.

"Next time, if you invite me, sure, lunch is on you. But seeing as *I* invited *you*, it's on me."

"Fair enough." He pushes his glasses up the bridge of his nose with a smile. "So how's the article coming along?"

"Good, really good, I think."

"You think, huh?"

"Well, I won't know for sure until you read it, will I?" Then for whatever reason, I decide to really stick my foot in my mouth. "You'll see it soon enough. Anyway, how was volleyball?"

My curiosity has been driving me crazy since I heard him on the phone with Rachel. As a friend and friend only, I need to know what and how that even came to be.

"It was good, great actually. We won the tournament."

"You and Rachel?"

His eyes crinkle at the corners while his mouth curls slyly to the side. "Now how would you know that?"

"Like you didn't know I was listening this morning." I lean forward a bit and then ask, "So it's true then? You and Rachel? How did that happen?"

He goes to answer but is interrupted by the server bringing us our lunch. His, a giant burger called "The Godfather," which is his all-time favorite thing to eat. And mine, a grilled chicken breast sandwich with a side of sweet potato fries. They both look absolutely mouthwatering, so we dig right in.

"So?" I ask impatiently after a couple more bites.

"So?"

"You were telling me about Rachel."

"Was I? I'm pretty sure you asked about the tournament first."

I sigh in mock frustration. "Fine, tell me about the tournament."

"We killed it actually," he says this with a huge grin. "She's really good, you should see her play."

For a second I'm nervous that he's looking to permanently replace me from the expression on his face. It's a cross between proud and smug. Before I even tackle that part of the Rachel issue, I have to know how he even thought about calling on her to sub for me in the first place. And why hasn't he said a word about it until I asked?

Oh my God, I'm turning into nosy Mimi.

This can't be good. But here goes nothing.

I reach for a fry and stuff it in my mouth while I'm asking, "Are you guys dating?"

But it comes out sounding like a bunch of mangled jargon.

Dylan's eyebrows inch together as he tries to decipher what I just asked him. It's cute to see him so confused. I can tell the moment he gives up because he puts down his burger, then wipes his mouth. Carefully setting his napkin on the table, he asks, "What did you just say?"

Afraid to ask again, I go to grab a fry and use the same technique to hide behind. But he leans across the small table and reaches out to gently take my wrist in his hand.

"Fine," I say, defeated. "Are you guys dating now?"

"Why do you ask?"

"We're friends, right?" I ask. He looks confused by my question but nods anyway.

"What does us being friends have anything to do with Rachel?"

I lean forward until my face is inches from Dylan's. At this distance, I get an up-close-and-personal look at his eyes. For the first time in all the time I've known him, I have to admit to myself that I can get a little lost in them. They're so bright, like an open field of fresh cut grass in Ireland. Not that I've ever been to Ireland, but the pictures I've seen obviously do it enough justice since it's stayed with me so vividly. Now I'm picturing myself running up a hill onto said random field. And then my arms go out wide and I spin and spin like Julie Andrews and sing to the sky for no reason whatsoever.

"Katy?"

I blink a couple of times. "Yeah."

He shakes his head with a smile at my momentary break with reality. I watch his eyes go to where he's touching me, and then he lets go of my wrist. "To answer your question, no, we're not technically dating."

Inwardly, I'm relieved. But that still doesn't quench my curiosity of how he ended up with Rachel on Saturday. I sit back in my seat a little more comfortably and decide not to ask anything else about it. Dylan, after a second or two, goes back to eating his lunch, so it would seem that the subject is dead and buried. However, in my head, that's a whole other story. I see them together: Holding hands, and everything seems innocent at first. Then the vision explodes into this flash of images of him pulling her close to him and kissing her. No, that's not quite right either. He's ravaging her mouth as her hands thread and pull wildly at his hair. My pulse trips in my throat as the images keep on coming. Each one more vivid than the one before it.

What is wrong with me? Why am I thinking about this? And why the hell does it bother me to the point that I'm embarrassed to even look at him right now.

It's not like I have never been around Dylan when he's dating someone. But as Mimi so thoughtfully brought up recently, he hasn't dated anyone in long while. And why is that exactly? Now that I'm thinking on it, we haven't discussed other people too much lately . . . ever, if I'm being honest about it with myself. That bothers me even more. Because what kind of best friends don't share those parts of their lives with each other? Not very good ones, I think. If it were Mimi, I'd tell her everything. Then again, she would probably force me to anyway. But with Dylan, it's different . . . it's always been different, hasn't it?

When I lock eyes with him across the table, it's as if he's trying to hijack the thoughts running through my mind. The ones that are chock-full of him and Rachel. I wonder if he can tell how much it bothers me, how much I don't want to admit that it does, and how much I wish being with him right now didn't feel off-kilter. Suddenly the table feels much smaller than it is. The sounds of the people around us one by one start to fall away until it's completely silent.

Then Dylan looks away and breaks the quiet. "How did it go with . . ." He searches his memory, then says, "Conner. How did it go on Saturday with Conner?"

As if a secret signal was radioed out from Gilbert's, my cell phone starts to vibrate on the table between us with an incoming call. The screen shows "Conner."

Dylan looks to the phone, then at me with a smile, and says, "Speak of the devil."

"I'll call him back later." And I go to silence it. But Dylan waves me off and tells me it's okay to take the call.

I manage to swipe the screen just in time and say hello.

"Did I catch you at a bad time, Shadow?"

I look at Dylan, who's now staring out the window, trying not to listen in to my conversation. Which is impossible to do since I'm sitting right across from him. His eyes shift to me and I hold up my finger and say to him, "I'll be off in a second."

"What was that?"

That comes from Conner.

"No, not you, I was talking to Dylan."

"Who's Dylan?" Conner asks.

"My boss. We're out to lunch."

"I'm sorry, I should let you go then."

I fidget in my seat a bit. "No, it's okay, what's up?"

"Well, I was wondering if you'd like to get together tonight. Maybe grab a bite to eat? If you're not busy or anything. If you can't make it, then—"

"I'm free," I quickly say and keep my eyes trained to the table. I can feel Dylan's heavy stare and realize that I shouldn't have taken a personal call in front of him as my boss. Even if we're friends, it's not professional. Then again, asking my boss if he's dating the office hottie isn't that professional either. But that's how we talk to each other. Always have.

Then why do I feel like a jerk for speaking to Conner in front of him? I know I shouldn't, but I do. What bugs me most about this is the fact that I can tell he senses it too. But if I know Dylan well enough, which of course I do, he won't bring it up. He'll go back to the usual best friend I've known for years. And then slip into boss role again while at the office . . . everything back to normal. Business as usual.

"Katy, are you still there?" Conner asks in my ear.

"Yes, I'm still here, sorry," I say in an embarrassed rush and pull my gaze away from Dylan. "Text me when and where and I'll meet you there."

"Sounds good. I'll see you later, Katy."

We say our good-byes and I put the phone on silent immediately afterward. Then, tucking it away into my bag, I say as if it wasn't obvious already, "That was Conner."

"Yeah, I could see that," Dylan says. "So I guess if you're making plans again, it went well over the weekend."

It registers then that Dylan thinks there is something between Conner and me. "Oh no, we're not old friends like *that*. We were best friends since we were kids. I haven't seen him in years, so we're just reconnecting until he goes back home to California."

"Then why did your face light up like the Fourth of July when he asked to meet you tonight?"

Did it?

It's possible, seeing as we are talking about Conner. But I don't think so. If anything, I felt very uncomfortable talking to Conner in front of Dylan. Which shouldn't happen, given our history. Actually, given both our histories, we should be able to talk about anything.

Jeez, at this rate, I'll be back at Jonathan's balcony sooner than later.

I try blowing it off like it's nothing. "I think you're imagining things."

"Fine, if you say so."

I do. I say so.

At least that's what I keep telling myself, hoping that it's nothing more than two friends catching up on old times.

We both go back to eating our lunches and return to talking shop. When we head back to the office, he goes his way and I go mine. I spend the rest of the day working on my article, and when Conner does text me the time and place eventually, I'm lucky Dylan is nowhere around to point out the ear-splitting grin that explodes across my face.

CHAPTER THIRTEEN

When I arrive at Bayview Park at six forty-five, I'm almost dripping in sweat. That's because after I received Conner's text to meet him at the park where we first met, I had just enough time to run home, change into some shorts and a run-of-the-mill T-shirt and sneakers, then run right back out and get here with fifteen minutes to spare.

I haven't been here in a while, so after parking my car by the tennis courts, I take the extra time while looking for Conner to appreciate it all. I walk the path that cuts around to the basketball court and then out to the open field that leads to the baseball diamond. I smile to myself when I turn around and head toward the playground, which is hidden from view since trees surround it now.

When I was a kid, most of those trees didn't exist, and I could see straight from the bottom of the slide across the field and then some. That's how my brothers were always able to keep an eye on me from pretty much wherever they were in the park at any given time.

It's also where I asked Conner to meet me one night nine or so years ago to give him the letter that I had poured all of my heart into. And it crosses my mind why he would pick to meet me here of all places. Actually, the thought has been in the forefront of my mind since he texted me this afternoon.

Just when I reach the now beautifully redone, brightly colored playground area, my phone vibrates in my back pocket.

I pull it out and see Dylan's text.

What was the nickname of Miami's first major league pro football team?

I text back with a huge smile, because this one is way too easy and I almost feel like my intelligence is being insulted.

Miami Seahawks

He texts me back within seconds:

We need to put you up against The Schwab, because this is ridiculous.

Laughing out loud at his text, that I could possibly even compete with Howie Schwab—sports trivia genius extraordinaire—has me so distracted that I barely hear Conner call out to me.

"Katy! Over here!"

I look around until I find him. He's off to the right side of the playground, underneath the spotty trees that cover a couple of picnic tables. I walk over, feeling very self-conscious all of a sudden about the fact that he keeps his eyes on me the whole length of the way.

When I reach the clearing, I finally notice that behind him, on the picnic table he's perched on, is a whole spread of food, carefully packaged. If I had to guess, not by Conner, but by someone in the gourmet food business, since it's done with beautiful cellophane wrapping and ribbons.

"Wow, Conner! This looks amazing!"

"So you're impressed, right?"

"Yes, very." I step a little closer to and say, "All of this is for me?"

"Shadow, if you can eat all of this food, I'll be the one who's impressed."

Amused at the prospect of getting to taste all of this stuff, I reach across the table and try to peek inside one of the wrapped dishes. Conner reaches out and lightly smacks the back of my hand.

"Not yet," he says. Standing up, he goes to fish around in a big bag off to the side of the picnic table. He comes out with a football. Throwing it up once and catching it in his hands, he says, "You've got to earn it. Are you ready? Do you think you can keep up?"

I put down my bag, then take the twisty band from my wrist and pull up my hair in a messy ponytail. "The better question would be do you think *you* can keep up with *me*?"

"I distinctly remember keeping up just fine, Katy."

"Yeah, but you're an old man now, so I'll probably get the jump on you."

He's almost doubled over laughing at my prediction. Albeit a bad one, because sure, I may still play volleyball every so often and run here or there in my spare time, but I haven't played any kind of actual football in a while. But in order to play football, all it really takes is a belief that you can; you have to convince yourself that you cannot be beaten, no matter what. If not, you might as well not even try.

He tosses me the ball, and I catch it easily. But I'm worried because I didn't wear a sports bra. It's not like he could've warned me that I would need it. Plus, how would that conversation even go? *Katy, make sure you strap your boobs down so they don't hurt.*

We walk into the clearing where other people are playing with their kids and their dogs. They're scattered around and enjoying the beautiful early evening weather, so we blend right in.

Quickly, we get the lay of the land and the amount of space we have to work with. He points to two specific groups of people on each side of us and anoints them as our out-of-bounds guide. Then I look over his shoulder and find the one tree far enough away to be considered the end zone.

"Okay, so I'll throw you a screen pass, then give you up to three Mississippi," he says, putting his hands out so I can toss him the ball back. "When I catch you, you're going to regret wearing white."

I look down at my mostly white T-shirt and then back up at Conner with a roll of my eyes. "Please, *if* you catch me is more like it."

"If that's how you want to play it, fine." He stands at our imaginary starting line and then motions to his left, where I'm supposed to be. "Are you ready?"

I get myself into a ready-to-take-off-and-run-the-hell-off-into-the-distance stance and then nod instead of answering out loud.

Conner shouts out a quick, "Ready, set, go," then volleys the ball into my waiting arms. And I'm off. My ponytail is swinging back and forth and swishing so loud that I can barely hear him counting down. But soon I can hear him running behind me.

With every step I get closer to our end zone, he's gaining ground. I hear him laughing behind me, though, as soon as I cross the line and spike the ball.

He slows his run down and stops beside me. We're both leaned over and have our hands on our knees, breathing heavily. When I look up at Conner, he's got that familiar smirk on his face. "I wasn't running at full speed. Figured I'd let you have one."

In the background, a random woman's voice yells out, "Girl power!"

I crack up and then toss the ball back to Conner. "Two out of three? So I can prove once and for all who is the better player and end this right here, right now."

"You're on, Shadow."

We trot the rest of the way back to the starting line and get ourselves into position. In my mind, I can already envision myself easily beating Conner, so I snicker at him as if we were little kids all over again. Then I get myself back into kicking-his-ass mode and put on the straight face. He chuckles at how serious my face gets and, I think, at how serious I'm taking this little impromptu competition. Which only serves to get me just the right amount of ticked off to make sure I beat him this time again.

Before long, Conner lobs me the ball and counts down. Then I'm sprinting for all I'm worth down the open field, closer to the sideline this time. And not too long after that, he's right on my heels. A lot closer this time around.

I'm so close I can taste it and the victory dance is already running through my head when Conner pops the ball out of my grasp from behind and tries to steal it. We're both in a tangle of arms and legs, trying to grab the football that is bouncing in between us in midair, until we both fall down on the ground. Thankfully, we weren't running at full speed anymore, so the fall isn't that bad. It's the way we land that's the problem.

I'm on my back, my hands above my head, holding on to the tip of the football for dear life. Conner is on top of me, straddling my hips, and reaching forward to grab the ball. It would all be fun and games if there wasn't this underlying tension that, yes, Mimi was correct, starts to build up between us. And when he goes to make a final grab at the ball, he stills his movements, looking down at me without saying a word.

I'm so close that I can see my reflection in his hazel eyes, which are staring right back at me. A chunk of his tousled light brown hair falls forward then and onto his forehead. And it takes everything in me not to reach up and push it aside for him. His eyes then veer their course and look down at my lips for the briefest of moments, making me want to pull him down closer . . . and closer still. But just as quickly as I catch him doing this and just as quickly as our previously rapid breathing slows to an almost trancelike rate, he sits up an inch or two and breaks the spell.

Then we hear the same random woman's voice from earlier yell, "Kiss her!"

He chuckles heartily at that and shakes his head while I completely ignore it.

And then everything seems to go right back to the way it was. He stands up and gives me a hand to help me off the ground. I pretend that didn't just happen and start to dust myself off.

"You've got something right . . ." He comes a step closer. His hand reaches out and into my hair, carefully pulling out a leaf. "There. Got it."

He holds the leaf and starts to spin it in between his fingers, mesmerized by it for a beat, then looks up at me and says my nickname once, as if remembering I'm still there.

"Yeah?" I ask cautiously.

"I think it's time we stop playing games." He tosses the leaf onto the ground and takes my hand in his with a big grin. "You've earned your keep. Let's eat."

CHAPTER FOURTEEN

When I leave Conner a couple of hours later, my head is spinning. It's not that the rest of the time with him had any other uncomfortable moments; in fact, it's the opposite. The problem is that neither of us acknowledged what almost happened, which is driving me crazy.

Because there is no doubt in my mind he was absolutely, one hundred percent about to kiss me when he had me pinned to the ground. As a woman, you just know these things. You don't have to be a rocket scientist to figure it out. Kind of how Jonathan described it: if he's attracted to you, you'll be able to tell.

And Conner is, without a doubt, attracted to me.

But he's not sold on the idea. It's almost as if he catches himself and remembers that it's me, Shadow, Katy, whatever. It's his childhood friend that he finds attractive all of a sudden and he doesn't really know what to do about it. Although, I could very well just be imagining all of it.

The look in his eyes was too full of want and temptation. And when his eyes zeroed in on my lips, I swear I could almost taste his lips against mine. My heart was hammering at about a thousand beats per second, waiting for a moment to happen that in the past I'd wanted so much. In the back of my mind, I was already dismissing the concern that he'd be going home soon. But time was nothing but a momentary roadblock keeping me from fulfilling my teenage dreams,, consequences be damned.

We left things light between us, almost too casual. We left things as if nothing happened and everything was A-OK, tentatively making plans for later in the week since the next couple of days I'll be on a deadline. This was fine by him since he had some things to take care of too.

Instead of driving home, I head over to the restaurant Mimi works at to take my mind off of things with Conner for a while. She'll have plenty to say about everything that happened today with Conner . . . and for that matter, with Dylan too. Because that whole Rachel business is still bugging me.

When I pull into the parking lot of Canyon Café, I immediately spot Simon's police cruiser. Great, just what I need today: a big heaping dose of Big Brother is Watching. How did he even know I was planning on heading over here? It's like he has a sixth sense or something where I'm concerned.

I stroll into the bar area to find Simon leaning against it and Mimi on the other side facing off with him. He's grinning from ear to ear, while her arms are folded and she's in a stance that screams that she's pissed.

"What's going on here?" I pull up a chair to watch the fireworks. "What did you say to her?"

"Me?" Simon points to himself with a dry laugh, then points to Mimi. "I don't know what her problem is. I come in here to see if she knows where you are, and she gives me an attitude."

"Oh please, you are so full of shit," Mimi says.

"I'm full of shit?" he asks her.

She leans into the bar, her eyes going soft and warm. If I didn't know that she loathes Simon, I'd think that she was about to grab his face and start kissing him senseless. In a sweet voice, she says, "You are so full of shit and you know it, Simon."

"Can we not do this today?" I motion across what little space is left between them. "I'm not in the mood at all."

Simon breaks his stare down with Mimi, which clearly Mimi was going to win, as she always does, to glance in my direction. "Does every woman I know have a problem with me today?"

"So you admit you only know two women?" Mimi asks. "I already knew that you suck with the ladies, but thanks for confirming that."

Simon starts to say something right back to her, but I put my hand up again. "Seriously, guys. Not tonight."

"Fine." They say in unison.

Mimi backs off the bar and turns her attention to me. She tilts her head to the side as she inspects me, trying to guess what could possibly have me in such a mood.

"Something happened today, didn't it?" she asks finally, after too long of a silence. "Which one?"

"Which one what?" Simon asks.

"None of your business," she says to Simon without sparing him a glance. Then, turning to me, she reaches across the bar and taps my hand with her index finger softly. "Hey, are you okay?"

"Katy, what the hell is going on?" Simon's voice is slightly frustrated now.

"Ignore him, okay?" Mimi says quietly to me. Then she looks over at him. "Simon, I'm going to ask you nicely so you know that I'm being serious. Please stop, turn around, and leave her alone."

Without a word, Simon turns on his heel and walks out of the bar as if under a magic spell. If I wasn't here to witness it myself with my own eyes, I wouldn't believe it.

"Wow, that actually worked," I say, still watching the doors he walked through and then looking back to Mimi in awe. "Why haven't we tried that tactic before?"

She waves her hand through the air as if it was nothing. "Forget about him. What's going on with you?"

"How can you tell?"

"It's my job as your best friend to be able to read you like a book. Trust me, Katy, I can tell something is up."

"Can I have a shot of Jameson?"

Her eyebrows fly so high up on her forehead that it looks like she doesn't have any to begin with. "What was that?"

"I *said*, can I please have a shot of Jameson?" I ask again.

"Okay, no, I definitely heard you right, it's just . . . well, I don't think I've ever seen you take a shot of anything."

"Well, there's a first time for everything."

"Apparently." She mumbles this as she reaches underneath the bar. With dexterity that comes from years of bartending and studying Tom Cruise in *Cocktail*, she tosses a bottle of amber liquid in the air and catches it. Then she puts a shot glass in front of me and dips the Posi-Pour to the edge to start filling it. "Bottoms up."

"Bottoms up," I echo as I take it and bring it to my lips. Without hesitation, I kick it back and let the liquid burn my throat. My face winces slightly, and then I say, "Another, please."

Mimi moves the bottle off of the bar and puts it away. "Uh-uh, now you're officially scaring me. No more until I decide that you've earned it."

I laugh. "That's what Conner said."

"Conner said what now?" Mimi asks in a huff. "You know what? Why don't you start at the beginning instead of jumping into story time like I was actually there."

"Fine." I rub the heels of my hands against my weary eyes and start at the beginning. "Did you know that Dylan is seeing Rachel?"

"Rachel? As in Tits Magee Rachel?"

"The one and only."

"Are you sure?" she asks. "Because Dylan doesn't strike me as the type to be into all of that. Then again, even I'd like to motorboat her, so . . ."

"That's the thing, I'm not sure if he is or he isn't."

My mind veers off to my lunch with Dylan and how things were left unsaid and unexplained between us. And as disconcerting as it is that something could be going on between him and Rachel other than her subbing for me at volleyball, I feel ridiculous for having an issue with it at all.

Mimi snaps her fingers in front of my face. "Earth to Katy, come in, Katy."

"I'm having some trouble reconciling the fact that he's into her. It just doesn't seem like him, you know?"

"Mm-hmm, sure. Whatever you say."

"I mean, it's not just me, right? Even you think it's strange that he's into her."

"He's a red-blooded male," Mimi says. "The poor guy probably just wants some alone time with her rack to forget about you for a minute or two and how you're hanging out with Conner all of a sudden. I don't blame him one bit."

"Dylan hasn't even met Conner. There is no way that that can be true."

"He doesn't have to meet Conner to be jealous of him." She is momentarily distracted by another customer and fulfills their drink order before coming back to me. "So what actually happened today that has you like this?"

"I almost kissed Conner. Actually, he almost kissed me."

Mimi's eyes widen as she leans her elbows on the bar. "Almost? Like tongues on the outside with no lips touching almost kind of kissing or close-mouthed and friend-zoned kind of kissing?"

"Who kisses with tongues on the outside like that? That's gross!"

"Well, if you've got a cold sore or something on your lip, you have to get creative," she explains matter-of-factly.

My stomach turns picturing this. "That is disgusting, Mimi! Please tell me you've never done that!"

"No, no, of course not. Forget I mentioned it, go on with your story."

"Okay, yeah, fine, um . . . where was I?"

She puckers up her lips and smacks them together loudly.

"Yeah, that's right," I say. "He almost kissed me. I mean, he was like right there staring at my lips like I was the last drop of water in a dry desert, and then nothing. It was as if he changed his mind all of a sudden and stopped himself."

"Did you have bad breath?" she asks.

"What? No!"

"It wouldn't kill you to keep a mint in your back pocket. Just saying."

I wave her off. "It had nothing to do with my nonexistent bad breath. He just stopped himself."

"Maybe he didn't think it was the right time. Did you ever think of that?"

"I don't know, Mimi. It felt really weird to be pinned to ground underneath him and—"

She puts up her hand to stop me. "Stop! You failed to mention before that he was on top of you. How did that happen?"

"We were playing football at the park and he tackled me." Her hand starts to move as if egging me on, so I add. "And that's it, really. He tackled me and was straddling my hips. Then the next thing I know, he's leaning forward and staring at my lips like he was going to eat me alive. And then nothing! He stopped!"

She lets out a long whistle when I finish talking. "Damn, girl, you were busy today, huh?"

"You can say that again. It was definitely interesting."

Mimi rests her elbows on the bar, then says, "All right, first let's tackle Conner, shall we?"

"By all means."

"Katy, he's probably not sure how to treat you. I mean, he knows how to treat you as a friend, obviously, but as a woman he's attracted to, not so much. Let me ask you this . . . would you have let him kiss you?"

Again, the answer comes to me quickly. Yes, I would have. There is only so much your imagination can conjure until you want to try out the real thing. So I nod.

"Then you need to figure out if this is a one-time thing between the two of you or if either of you is looking for more. And more importantly, you're going to have to make the first move with Conner. He's too freaked out by the prospect that you're a grown-up and hot to be able to do it on his own. So you're going to have to bite the bullet if you want to finally see what he's like in the sack."

"Mimi, since when have you known me to make the first move?" She thinks on this for good couple of seconds, until I say, "Never, that's when."

"Well, there's always a first time for everything. Don't knock it until you try it."

I shake my head. "And that whole thing you said about wanting more . . . that would be impossible since he doesn't even live here."

"Stranger things have happened." Then she smiles and says, "Which brings us back to Dylan."

"Can you believe him and Rachel?" I ask again, still genuinely surprised by this development. "I still can't wrap my head around it."

"Oh, Katy, Katy, Katy." She props her chin up with her hand and grins like an idiot at me for a beat. "You don't have a problem with Dylan and Rachel being together. That is, if they're even really together or going to be together or whatever the hell they are."

"I don't?" I ask, relieved that she thinks this.

"No, you don't," she says softly. "Your problem is seeing Dylan with *anyone*. It doesn't matter if her name is Rachel or not. You're jealous. End of story. And the sooner you admit this to yourself, the sooner we can move on to how you're going to deal with Dylan in your life. Because, sweetie, he's in your life . . . but you need to be careful with him."

"Careful? Why do I need to be careful with him?"

"He cares a lot about you and has for a long time," she answers as I'm saying no to her, but she shushes me quickly. "Katy, you can really hurt him the most in all of this, so please, just be careful with him."

"I would never hurt Dylan, that's ridiculous."

"Sometimes we don't mean to hurt the ones we love, but we do anyway."

"I'm not jealous of Rachel and I certainly am not *in love* with Dylan, Mimi." She raises an eyebrow at this and smacks her lips together as if I am boring her now. "I care about him, of course. A lot, as a friend . . . but that's it. And as a friend, I don't want to see him with someone *like* Rachel. Just like I wouldn't want to see you with the male equivalent of Rachel."

She stares at me with a knowing smile and doesn't say another word. When her mouth drops open to finally give me more of what's on her mind, I'm saved by the bell. A couple strolls into the bar and decides to sit one seat over from me, forcing Mimi to give them her undivided attention immediately. I take the opportunity to sneak off my bar stool and start gathering my things to leave.

"Chickenshit," Mimi mumbles under her breath.

"Me? I'm not the one dating someone in secret," I say with a sly smile, and then she squints her eyes at me. "Yeah, don't think I've forgotten about that. Good night, Mimi."

"Yeah, good night to you too."

My back is to her when she says this, so I raise my hand and wave to her, already making my way to the door. I need to get home and hide under the blankets and figure out what I'm going to do about Conner . . . and Dylan. Maybe tomorrow I'll get a do-over. But once I'm in bed, my thoughts become a jumble of images that range from Dylan with faceless women to Conner actually kissing me for the first time. It's that last thought that brings a memory still as vivid today as it was when it actually happened. And this time I don't need the letter to remind myself how painful it was when he rejected me.

CHAPTER FIFTEEN

Nine years ago . . .

I had been waiting on the swings for Conner for what felt like hours. But it really was only a few minutes. He'd said he would be here at dusk when I called him earlier. At first he'd seemed hesitant to meet me. Which made sense since we hadn't been hanging out together as much lately.

Since Conner was a senior in high school and approaching the end of his time here before heading off to college, he'd been even more busy than usual. We had barely spoken to each other in the last few months. What with prom, his new friends, and packing for college, it was next to impossible to spend any time together.

But that didn't lessen the feelings I had for him. They were growing more and more each day. And on the rare occasions that we were together lately, my nervousness around him made it impossible to act like myself. My mind was consumed with Conner.

I was in love with him.

I had been since the day he carried me off the soccer field at tryouts a couple of years ago. When I look back, I think that maybe I had been falling in love with him a little bit each day before then. But that one day changed everything.

Because I suddenly understood what all those stupid love songs were about. How one look, one breath, one touch could change your life forever. How one person could be the person for you and you could forget everyone else.

That's how I'd been.

I was sixteen years old and had never even been kissed. I'd come close, but couldn't do it. In my heart and soul, I wanted Conner to be my first kiss and first . . .

My heart started to thump away in my chest, thinking about him being that close to me, wanting me as much as I wanted him. I felt as if I'd just received a shot of adrenaline as I pictured myself being on the receiving end of Conner's affection. The affection that I knew for a fact he'd already given to a couple of girls. Older girls . . . more mature girls.

But that night, after much thought on my part, I'd decided that I'd finally tell him how I'd been feeling. That he'd see for himself how much I'd matured and how much I wanted this to happen. I needed to do this now, before it was too late and he was gone.

Absentmindedly, I pulled the letter I had spent the better part of three days writing out of my back pocket. The paper felt heavy in my hands. I'd known that seeing Conner face-to-face tonight would be difficult enough and that saying the words out loud would have been next to impossible. So I'd decided to put pen to paper instead. He'd read the letter and know everything.

Every little thing I wanted to happen between us. And every little thing I'd been feeling about him.

Anticipation and anxiety gnawed away at me as I heard the familiar groan and squeak of Conner's brakes somewhere in the near distance. There was no turning back now. This was it. Within seconds he'd be standing right in front of me and I'd hand him the letter.

What if he laughed at me?

I tossed that thought out of my head as quickly as it materialized. There was no way the Conner I knew would laugh at me. I just needed to stay calm and stop doubting myself.

Hurriedly, I stuffed the letter back into my pocket when I heard his footsteps getting closer in the near darkness of the park. With each step he took, my heart beat faster and faster until my ears heard nothing but a steady hum of white noise. And then he was there, standing a foot or two away from me.

He was much taller now. He might have been even taller than the last time I saw him. Even in the dimly lit park, I could see a small smile slowly pulling at the corners of his mouth. His handsome, strong jaw had a little more scruff than usual, and it made him look older than his eighteen years.

"Hey there, Shadow," he said.

"Hey."

Inwardly, I winced at the nickname. In the first few years of our friendship, it had been cute and kind of funny to hear him refer to me by it. But lately, I'd wanted him to call me by my name. And for a second or two I thought I'd made a huge mistake by asking him to meet me here. Because I was afraid that he'd never see me as anything other than his shadow.

Conner took the empty swing seat beside me, studying me at the same time. He noticed that something wasn't quite right and stayed quiet as I lazily dragged my feet in the dirt beneath me. I was trying to work up the courage to say why I had asked him to meet me here. But instead, a fear so strong took hold of me and kept me from talking.

He cleared his throat and started to swing, kicking his legs and using his weight to make himself get higher. The swing set rocked with the force of him and he started laughing. Then, as he swung backward so fast he was like a blur in the night, he said, "Come on, Shadow. Let's see who can go higher for old times' sake."

A part of me wanted it to be like it was when we first met and just swing away all night with him. But I couldn't let myself go back there. So I stayed where I was and watched him until he slowed down and finally came to a stop.

"Are you okay?" he asked. "You haven't said two words since I got here."

"I . . ." I paused, nervously searching for the right words. "I need to talk to you."

Conner's eyebrows knit together. "So something is wrong? What happened?"

"No, there's nothing wrong. I promise."

"Are you sure?" His eyes searched mine for a hint that I might be lying. "Did you get in trouble or something?"

I shook my head and managed to smile at him. And I knew in that instant that the words would not come, that the letter would have to do the talking for me. So without much fanfare, I reached for it and pulled it out of my back pocket once again. It crinkled in my hand as I held it between us. His hazel eyes, which looked almost green in the moonlight now, shone brightly as he looked from the letter to me.

Shakily, I said, "I wrote you a letter."

"Shadow," he said with a chuckle, "you know I'm not leaving for college until the end of the month, right? I think that's when you're supposed to start writing me letters."

"Just take it."

Conner was still smiling when he reached out and took the letter. He immediately went to shove it into the back pocket of his jeans.

"I want you to read it right now," I said. "Please."

The serious tone in which I said this must have been enough, since Conner nodded and took the letter in his hands. Carefully, he unfolded the creases and held it in front of him. In this area of the park it was a little difficult since it was now almost pitch-dark, but he finally managed to see enough that he could start reading.

I held my breath as he read quietly. I tried unsuccessfully to not look at him too. His face was smooth of emotion. He gave away nothing as he continued reading. And when he turned the page over, knowing exactly where in the letter he was at that point, I could feel my stomach drop to around my ankles. I sneaked another glance at him as he neared the end and read *what I was asking of him. He just kept staring at the paper in his hands in what looked like disbelief.*

And I knew right then that he didn't feel any of the same things I felt for him. I knew that I shouldn't have done this and that our friendship was never going to be what it was. Worst thing of all, I couldn't take any of it back.

After a beat, he handed me back the letter and said something that I'll never forget. "I wish you hadn't written this, Shadow."

My heart already breaking, I felt like it splintered in my chest into a million pieces. I struggled to maintain eye contact with him and failed. Those eyes of his would always read me like an open book. So I wondered how it was that he hadn't seen this coming. How he couldn't see that this girl was in love with him and had been saving herself for him. It was as if he refused to see me as anything other than his sidekick. And it hurt me deeply to know that it would always be that way between us.

I crumpled the letter and stood up. The hurt I felt bubbling underneath the surface broke as tears started to fall from my eyes. But I managed to say one more thing to him. In fact, it was the very last thing I ever said to him before he left for college.

"You know what, Conner? I wish I had never written you this letter too."

I meant it as much as I didn't. I mean, I never meant for us to literally just stop talking to each other. But I knew that it wouldn't have been the same, what with me having offered him my virginity and my undying love. Ashamed and hurt, I quickly walked out of the park and farther away from him. I could hear him calling after me. But I didn't dare turn around.

It was done.

And I would have to live with the consequences.

CHAPTER SIXTEEN

With my deadline looming, I'm occupied for the next couple of days.

I barely have time to say a quick hi and good-bye to Mimi when I leave the apartment in the morning and come home at night. Thankfully, she's used to my schedule by now and doesn't hold it against me. Plus, she's busy with bartending, design school, and her mystery man, so she has plenty on her plate to juggle.

But once Wednesday afternoon rolls around and I've confirmed all my sources for the umpteenth time and have done a revision followed by another revision of the article . . . I'm finally happy with it. I press Send on my iPad and off it goes to Dylan's inbox for review.

After I submit an article to Dylan, I always pop my head up to look across the newsroom into his office. If the windows that face out to the bullpen are open, I try to read his expression. It never really works from this far away, but it's a habit at this point. When I glance toward his office now, I see that the blinds are drawn for privacy, but the door is open. And this time, I find Rachel's back to me, leaning with purposeful casualness against his door.

My excitement is quickly replaced by . . .

Shit.

Nope, I'm not feeling any twinge or even the slightest hint of jealousy. Not going to give in to the rush of adrenaline coursing through my veins right now while the very clear image of me kicking Rachel's shins flashes across my mind.

I cannot be jealous. This really can't be happening. I've never felt anything like this when it comes to Dylan before. Since I've known him for so long, I'm well aware of the women he's dated or had flings with . . . and never once, in all of that time, have I ever felt like this.

Right then, Rachel giggles at something he must have said. I know this because I'm still staring like a hawk with laser eyes. As I continue to pretend-shoot her with laser beams, I find myself saying things under my breath like, "Really?" "Seriously?" "Oh, now you remember that your top button isn't buttoned. How convenient."

That last one happens when Rachel realizes that her blouse is missing a button or something. She looks over her shoulder in fake embarrassment and down to her breasts. Then she turns around and, before the rest of the newsroom, proceeds to button not one, but two, two buttons! She giggles one more time—I think I'm going to be sick—and then turns around to continue whatever the conversation was before her boobs were flying out of her top, giving Dylan a very extensive view.

That's it. Not being able to take this torture any longer, I head to his office. My intention is to interrupt them so that she will scurry off to her upstairs cubicle and hopefully not come back down until the next millennium.

I'm almost right behind her when I hear Phoebe's lifeless and no-nonsense voice break through my senses.

"May I help you, Ms. Lewis?"

Rachel uncrosses her ankles and stands up straighter, adjusting her skirt before turning around to give me a look that if I didn't know any better, would make me think that she was the love child of Phoebe and Satan.

From somewhere in his office, Dylan asks, "Katy, is that you?"

Seemingly, my impromptu intervention worked, because Rachel says good-bye to him, but not before she lets us *all* know—and by all, I'm pretty sure it is for my benefit only—that he should call her later tonight. Then, as she struts right by me, she whispers for only me to hear, "He's all yours."

"Ms. Lewis?" Phoebe asks once Rachel is completely gone.

I struggle to make my next move, so rattled with nerves and anxiety that I don't respond. I stand there like a deer in headlights. Because what did I just do? More importantly, *why* did I just do it?

How am I supposed to act around him now?

Admit it, Katy, you're officially jealous.

"I can't be," I mutter out loud to myself.

"Mr. Sterling," Phoebe says. "I believe your friend is incapacitated at the moment. Please retrieve her."

It's like I'm there but not there. It's as if I'm hyperaware that my body and mind are all connected like they teach you in grade school: *The knee bone's connected to your thigh bone. The thigh bone's connected to your hip bone.*

The lyrics dance around in my head until Dylan appears in his doorway. I forget the song and focus solely on him and . . . Jesus, his eyes are so amazingly beautiful. Like two emerald pools to get lost in forever and ever and a day.

"Katy?"

I smile at him, trying my hardest not to let it show that what I did with Rachel was complete sabotage. The smile stretches on and on, making me feel like my face might split in two if I don't stop anytime soon.

"Hey, so did you read the article?" I ask, pretending like nothing happened. Still smiling like a loon. "I sent it over to you."

He adjusts his glasses while looking at the carpet and then back up at me, shaking his head with a chuckle. "I know you sent it . . . like two minutes ago. I was busy."

"Do you mind if I sit in while you read it?" I ask.

He thinks about it for a second, then says, "Sure, come in."

Dylan steps aside to let me walk into his office, where I sit in one of his leather wingback chairs as he closes the door. They're closer to the floor-to-ceiling windows that line his office on the far side and overlook downtown Fort Lauderdale. The view is breathtaking, and I'm completely wrapped up in it while I hear him get settled behind his desk again. It's enough to distract me from the overwhelming feeling that I'm coming across like an idiot and helps to calm my nerves.

After a few moments of silence, he says, "It's good, Katy. Do you want to run it as is? Or do you want to add anything else to it?"

Still looking out the window, I tell him to run it as is.

Then I hear him stand up and walk over to me. He crouches beside the chair and waves his hand in front of my face to get my attention.

"Sorry," I mumble. "I think I'm really tired or something. It's been a long few days."

He stands up and then leans against the window, putting his hands in his pants pockets and crossing his legs at the ankles. This makes me cringe every single time he does it. Because I don't care if they are the sturdiest windows in the free world, they're freaking windows! They can shatter into pieces and down goes Dylan, flying to the ground.

I go back to staring out the window, keenly aware that he's watching me. I search myself for the answer to what brought me over to his office in the first place. Is it that I'm truly jealous of Rachel? Or is it something more than that? Has Mimi been right all this time about Dylan caring about me a lot more than he's let on? Hell, maybe she's been right about me carrying some sort of torch for him too. Do I? I feel like the world's biggest jerk, but I don't even know if that's true. All this time he's been right there, always supporting me, always caring about me . . . and vice versa. How do I know where the friendship ends and something else begins?

The questions come one right after the other and not one answer is clear. Which scares me to death. Because if I lose Dylan . . . I don't know what I'd do.

Out of nowhere, he asks, "Is it about Conner?"

"Huh?" I look up at Dylan. His face is expressionless, as usual. Which makes this all even more confusing.

"Does the way you're acting have anything to do with Conner?"

"Why would you think that?"

He shrugs his shoulders. "I don't know. Maybe it's the fact that you don't talk about him easily with me. You've never been that way before."

Is that true? If it is, it's not intentional. In the past, I've been able to talk about exes openly with him. Although with my last boyfriend, Bailey the dream killer, it became a little difficult toward the end of our relationship. Because Dylan didn't care for Bailey one bit, I purposely withheld a lot of details from him, knowing that it would only make him upset. But even I have to admit that the timing of Conner's visit is a bit too much for me to handle. Even though I'm usually able to compartmentalize each part of my life, this predicament is making it nearly impossible for me to think straight half the time. As evidenced by the Rachel debacle a few minutes ago. The normal Katy wouldn't toy with the idea of doing something so crazy as purposely keeping her from him. Who in their right mind would?

Then, for whatever reason, I decide to test the boundaries with Dylan. It's not my finest moment, but something in me wants to prove that I'm not jealous of Rachel . . . that I don't want Dylan in any other way than a friend.

"Actually, yeah, there is something going on with Conner, but I'm not sure you're going to want to hear about it. It's kind of embarrassing."

His jaw tightens, and then almost as quickly as it happens, he releases the tension around his face and smiles halfheartedly. "I'm sure it's not that embarrassing."

I lean forward in my seat. "Do you promise not to laugh?"

He runs his finger up and then across his heart.

I can just stop talking and end it right here. I can pretend that I'm not the least bit curious as to what he'll think or say. But the irrational side of me wants to push the boundaries.

"I don't think I'm that kissable."

Dylan nearly chokes and starts to cough, covering it up. "What did you say?"

"Dylan, I'm serious. There must be something I'm doing wrong because Conner won't kiss me. I thought it was the perfect moment the other day, but nope, he didn't do it. So it must be me."

"It's not you," he says and then runs a hand down his face as if it will help to clear his thoughts. "Maybe he's just nervous around you. Did you ever think of that?"

"I guess. But what if—"

"No, Katy, there is no what if. Trust me, he's probably nervous."

I'm standing and take a step toward him before I can change my mind. The look on his face is somewhere between trancelike and confused. In turn, he stands up straighter and pulls his body away from the window.

"Can you tell me if I did something wrong?" I ask in as friendly a voice I can muster. "Like do I have bad breath?"

"How can I tell you if you did something wrong?"

As soon as he says this, my meaning clicks for him by the look of surprise on his face. Which is better for me, so I don't have to come right out and explain.

"Just tell me if I did something wrong, okay?"

Dylan stays completely still and quiet. If I couldn't see the steady beat of his pulse on the side of his neck, I would swear that he was dead. It's bad enough that my heart is jackhammering away inside its cage in my chest, making it nearly impossible to stay as calm on the outside as I'm trying to be in front of him.

It's a test, that's all this is. Get it over with so you can move on.

I'm thinking this while reaching out to take Dylan's hands in mine. He doesn't resist, so that's good. Then he lets me position them on my waist, leaving them there when I take my hands away. I feel a charge of excitement run through me at the warmth of his hands against my body. And it frightens me a little. So I keep my eyes trained on his throat and watch in fascination as it bobs up and then down, as if he is swallowing a breath. Not having to look in his eyes is enough to propel me an inch forward and loop my arms around his neck.

"Katy?"

He says this so quietly that I can't tell if it's a plea or a question. So I move closer until our bodies are pressed together, like we're about to start a slow dance. I've finally been able to clear my mind of all stray thoughts and focus on this moment, right here, right now, that I know will change everything. But I still can't gather the nerve to look up at him, because if I do, I already know I won't be able to stop.

In a voice so low, I ask, "If you were this close to me, like you are now, would you want to kiss me?"

He doesn't answer, but I can tell that his breathing is becoming more rapid by the way his chest rises and falls. So I ask him again.

It's then he moves his hand off my waist and underneath my chin to tip my face up to look at him. He skims over my features with his eyes until reaching my lips, where he holds them in his gaze for a moment too long to be considered merely friendly.

Then quietly, he says, "Yes."

"Yes, what?"

"Yes, I would kiss you."

For a split second, I want him to kiss me right now. The feeling is so overwhelming that my lips actually ache with the need to have his mouth against mine. And for a second or two, I sense that he's struggling with the same thought. But then Dylan drops his hands away and lets them fall to his sides as if remembering the boundaries of our relationship. I step back and smile as best I can while a hurricane of emotion rolls inside of me.

The silence between us grows thicker with unanswered questions while I walk backward. I move farther and farther away from him, then my back finally hits his office door. My body rests against it for a second or two until I reach behind me to turn the knob. I already know that when I walk out of this room, the friendship I have with Dylan will not be the same. I also know that the look on his face is one of the saddest I've ever seen on him. And it confirms everything I didn't want to believe until today.

He's in love with me.

CHAPTER SEVENTEEN

For the past few hours I've been sitting on my couch, staring into oblivion and replaying over and over what happened with Dylan earlier today.

When I practically stormed out of his office, I stopped at my desk, collected my things, and mumbled something about going home sick to the nearest body, who was shocked to hear this. Me taking any kind of sick time is unheard of. I report to work and do my job even if I'm on my deathbed. But I needed to think. And to think clearly, I didn't want to be anywhere around Dylan, so I went home.

My cell phone has been vibrating left and right since I got here, but I haven't bothered to check it. I'm afraid to see if he's reached out to me. I'm terrified that I won't get my daily text. Because as silly as those texts are, they mean something to me.

It must be close to midnight when Mimi's keys jangle in the front door of the apartment. She takes one look at me on the couch, drops all of her things, and sits down beside me.

"What the hell happened that you're sitting here in the dark?"

I look around. "The kitchen light is on."

"You know what I mean. Is everything all right?"

"I almost kissed Dylan today."

I let that hang in the air between us. Because it's the first time I've said it out loud. Replaying it over in my head is one thing, but to admit it to someone else is quite another.

Mimi sits up as straight as an arrow and her mouth falls open in shock. "What?! How did that happen? And didn't you almost kiss Conner a couple of days ago?"

"Almost. I said I *almost* kissed him."

"Fine, you *almost* kissed him. How did that come to be? Did you fall into his lap or something?"

Tugging some hair behind my ear, I nervously tell her the story from start to finish. I don't bother to hide any of it, including the Rachel part, because what's the point? Mimi will get it out of me anyway, eventually.

When I'm done, I finally say, "I'm a horrible person, Mimi. I shouldn't have done that . . . any of it."

She hasn't said a word since I started, so I look at her from the corner of my eye. She's bouncing in her seat with excitement, and she's covering her mouth with her hand, looking like someone who just walked into their own surprise party.

"Would you please say something already!"

Her hand falls away from her mouth to reveal her lips in a perfect *O* shape. Then, after a few more silent seconds, she says, "I can't believe you had a fucking John Hughes moment today."

I'm about to ask what she means by this but she keeps on ranting.

"Do you know how many women wait to experience a John Hughes moment in their lives? It's probably in the millions. And you . . . you, of all people, not only pulled a John Hughes moment, you pulled one of the top three possible John Hughes moments to reenact." She reaches over in the middle of her speech and covers my hand with hers, then taps it gently with a mother's touch. "I'm impressed, Katy. But I'm also a little mad at you. Because I told you to be careful with Dylan . . . and the John Hughes moment you picked was probably the worst one to use on him."

"What are you even talking about?" I ask.

She's already up and running to her purse on the floor by the front door. When she's back, she's pressing some buttons on her phone and telling me to be quiet. "Shush! I need to find something."

"I'm in the middle of a crisis, Mimi. Your Twitter account can wait."

She freezes midtype and turns her attention to me. "I'll be tweeting about this shit later, for sure. But right now, I'm looking something up for you."

Then she's back typing away, and when she finds what she was looking for, she grabs my arm and pulls me closer to her. We're huddled over her phone while a scene plays out from a movie I haven't seen in years called *Some Kind of Wonderful*.

After the scene is over, I turn to Mimi and ask, "So I'm Watts in this scenario? Is that what you're saying?"

"Girl, I think you might as well have Watts stamped across your forehead. But you've also got a little of Keith going on too."

"Keith? How is that even possible?"

"Bear with me for a minute, okay?" She gets up from the couch and stands in front of me. Her hands go up, waving back and forth like she is going to do some kind of alternate version of show and tell. "Are you ready to have your mind blown?"

I have to laugh at her enthusiasm. "Sure, hit me."

"So, you've got Keith over here," she says and motions to her left. "He's been infatuated with Miss Amanda Jones pretty much all of his natural born life. Key word in that sentence is *infatuated* . . . because hello! Katy, let's face it, you're infatuated with Conner, so that one is easy to figure out."

"I was infatuated with him when we were kids, not anymore."

"Yeah, right, whatever you say. Moving on," she says, dismissing me. "Over here we've got Miss Amanda Jones." She pouts a little and with a whiny voice adds, "Poor little Amanda comes from the wrong side of the tracks and just wants to fit in with the rich kids. But for her to do that, she puts up with an utter dick . . . Hardy."

She freezes and looks like she has an epiphany. "What now?" I ask.

"Ohmygod, ohmygod! I am a genius! Rachel is Hardy!" she yells at the top of her lungs. "This is perfect!"

I rub my face with my hands, at this point lost in whatever she's trying to explain to me. "Mimi, get to the point already."

"Okay, so Watts is in love with Keith, but Keith is infatuated with Amanda, who's a bitch with a heart of gold and turns out to be a half-way decent human being."

"Are you saying that Rachel is a nice person?"

She puts her hands on her hips like the answer is obvious and says, "No. She's still a bitch. This is a movie we're talking about, Katy, not real people."

"But you just said I'm Watts and Keith and Rachel's Hardy and Amanda . . . wait, who is Amanda in all of this?"

Mimi thinks for a second on this, the wheels spinning in her head, trying to place this character into my actual life. "She's a metaphor."

I'm doubled over laughing and can't stop. A metaphor? A metaphor for what? So I ask her, because I'm sure she'll come up with something.

"She's a metaphor for all the things you can't have. Wait," she says suddenly. "No, no, no, that's not it. She's a metaphor for all the things you want but are afraid to ask for. Like Conner . . . like Dylan."

"Why would I be afraid?" I ask, my laughter dying down. "And what am I asking for?"

"To be loved by one of them, duh. Come on, Katy, you have to keep up or all of this is pointless."

"Fine, go ahead." I wave my hand toward her. "You have the floor."

"All right. So Watts, in helping Keith—her best bud who she's in love with—get with Amanda, lets it slip to Keith that what he's been looking for is not in Amanda but in her. And that Watts is his one and only . . . his soul mate, his forever." Mimi walks back to the couch and sits down, then she takes a big gulp of air. "Dylan let you pretend to practice or not practice a kiss on him because he's in love with you and would do anything to be close to you in that way. And you went ahead with it because deep down, I think you're really in love with Dylan and don't want to admit it. Then there's Conner, who is your first real crush from forever ago. Is he hot? Sure. But he's not the one. He's your 'what if?' . . . which is a big difference. Naturally, there is a part of you that wants to see what it's like to be with him or what could have been, but I guarantee that you'll be disappointed. Because in your heart of hearts, it's Dylan who is front and center. Oh, and Rachel and Hardy can go fuck themselves, by the way."

I rest my head on the couch and close my eyes. I picture the look in Dylan's eyes when he pulled my chin up. It was as if he wasn't hiding his true feelings anymore and wanted me to *really* see him for the first time as more than a friend. Then I see Conner in my mind's eye and how he made me feel when he was about to kiss me the other day. There was a sense of curiosity and lust swirling around his eyes as he struggled with the idea before letting the moment go.

"So, am I right? I'm right, aren't I?" Mimi asks.

"I think it's a little more complicated than all of that." I open my eyes and turn my head to look at her. "What am I going to do, Mimi?"

"I told you to be careful with Dylan."

"I know, I know," I say. "But I needed to do something to find out if I felt—"

"Jealousy, love, lust."

I chuckle. "Yes, all of those things."

"And?"

"And I still don't know what to do."

She thinks for a beat, then says, "Whatever you do, Katy, please don't hurt him . . . I don't think Dylan can take it much longer."

"I know."

Mimi gets up from the couch and starts to head to her bedroom. Before she disappears down the hallway, she turns and leans against the wall. "Look, do what feels right to you and don't second-guess yourself. If it's meant to be with Dylan, it will happen. Then again, if it's meant to be with Conner, it will happen. The question is which one do you want it to happen with more."

Then she disappears and says a good night to me before closing her bedroom door and leaving me to dwell on what she just said. What she forgot to mention, and what is making my stomach feel as if it were tied up in knots, is how do I not get hurt in all of this?

Finally, I give up on all of it, and when I'm too tired to think about any of it for a minute more, I take my cell phone out to check my messages.

I scroll through all the little text dialogue boxes without unlocking my phone . . . noticing with a lot more than disappointment that Dylan's daily trivia text isn't one of them. But there is one from Conner saying he'll meet me at the game Friday night and that he's looking forward to seeing me again.

I should be happy about this, and I am a little . . . but not as much as should be, I think.

Maybe if I wasn't so hung up on Dylan's missing text, I could muster more excitement over seeing Conner again.

Yeah, maybe . . . then again, maybe not.

CHAPTER EIGHTEEN

I manage to stay out of sight and under the radar of both Dylan and Conner the next day. Which is perfect since I have to get back to my actual life and go to the Barracudas' last practice of the week before their game tomorrow night. Is it a bit of a cop-out that I'm using my job as a way to avoid both of them? Sure, but I need it and I'll take it.

After practice, I realize that I left one of my journals at my desk in my rush to escape yesterday. So I check the time, thinking that the coast will be clear, specifically that Dylan won't be around and I can run in and out without being detected.

When I get to the office, most of the day staff is gone since it's already past seven o'clock. But the main newsroom floor is still buzzing with energy and enough people that I can duck in and make a beeline straight to my desk.

I don't even bother to pull off my messenger bag when I sit down and start looking for the journal in question. I could have sworn I left it on my desk yesterday, but I don't see it right away, so I start to open and close drawers. And that's when I notice the Butterscotch Krimpets stash . . . and that's when my stomach growls in response, reminding me that I've barely had a bite to eat today.

I give in and grab a pack, ripping it open and stuffing one into my mouth whole. As soon as the taste of butterscotch melts against my tongue, my eyes roll into the back of my head in ecstasy.

"Katy?"

When I hear Dylan's voice behind me, it startles me enough that I start to choke on the food I was trying to swallow. He smacks my back a couple of times to keep me from choking to death, and then once he sees that I'm okay, runs over to the water cooler to get me a cup.

Handing it to me, he asks, "What are you doing in here so late? I thought you were supposed to be at practice."

I take a quick gulp of water, trying very hard not to look up at him. I've already noticed he's got his laptop bag in tow and his keys in hand and was probably headed out the door when he spotted me.

"I just left the practice and stopped in for a second before heading home."

I quickly look in the final drawer in my desk and find the missing journal. I pull it out and hold it tight against my chest when I turn back around to face him.

"See, I was looking for this." I finally sneak a glance at his face.

This was a mistake, because Dylan looks like someone told him his dog was dead. And he doesn't even have a dog, but if he did, I bet he would look somewhere along the lines of how he does now.

His usually vibrant eyes are dull and lifeless, and his shoulders are slumped in defeat. He runs a hand through his dark hair and then goes to say something but stops. I'm afraid that what he will want to say is that I'm an awful person for playing with his emotions yesterday and every day before that. I'm scared that I can no longer be his friend, confidante, or colleague, even. And all of that terrifies me to death because I could never see a future that didn't include him in it in some capacity. Until now.

Instead of facing this giant divide between us head-on, because I'm too spooked at the idea of losing him and hearing him say it out loud, I go to leave. I get about two steps away from him when he calls out to me again.

"Do you mind if I come to the game tomorrow night?" he asks.

Genuinely caught off guard by his question, at first I don't say yes or no. Normally I wouldn't mind at all, but given the way the last few days have gone, I'm not so sure. And I know myself . . . I'll be distracted the whole time I'm trying to work, knowing that Dylan is around. But I don't want him to think that everything is ruined between us either.

"Of course not," I finally say to him. "I'll see you there."

He smiles a little, looking relieved that I'm okay with him being there. Which makes me feel only slightly better. I say a quick good-bye to him and try my hardest to walk more calmly out of the office than I did yesterday.

When I manage to clear the newsroom and get to the office elevator, I rest my head against the wall in frustration as it goes down to the parking garage. My frustration is self-made, though, which is the most maddening thing about it. I could have avoided all of this by not playing that little game with Dylan yesterday. It makes me sick to my stomach to know that I had a hand in this . . . a big one.

And what I want most is to fix things between us, I just don't know how.

———————

The Friday night lights are in full swing and I'm in my element: on the sidelines, watching the game, taking a few pictures and notes for my article. It's a welcome relief to be doing what I love most.

As much as I'm a bit biased while watching my old alma mater play their games live, I've been able to resist hinting that I'm a true-blue fan in my pieces. I stay completely neutral and report the facts. Like how they are losing by two touchdowns right now, heading into the second quarter.

A man's voice calls my name from somewhere behind me and I turn around to try to place it. But with the crowded bleachers and all the people on the field, it's impossible to make it out.

Then I distinctly hear, "Shadow," ring through the crowd noise. I turn, this time to my left, and spot Conner. It's hard not to. He's easily a foot taller than most of the high schoolers standing around him. I wave for him to come down to the field and he starts making his way to me.

I'd be a liar if I didn't admit to myself that I get a rush of butterflies seeing him again. I don't think there will ever be a time that I don't. He's such a big part of my past that it's next to impossible to imagine a day that my heart doesn't skip a beat or two at the mere idea of him.

"Well, don't you look adorable," he says by way of hello.

I look down at myself. Jeans, check. Ratty old Converse sneakers, check. Black hoodie sweatshirt, check. Hair up in a ponytail, check. Not sure why he would think this is adorable, but I get the smallest of thrills knowing it.

"Thanks."

And then I hesitate over what I should do next. Because I'm not sure if we should hug hello or kiss on the cheek after what happened at the park. It's times like these that I wish I knew exactly what Conner was thinking about me and not just my clothing choices. I would love to know if he's as confused as I am and doesn't know what he can say or do around me without it bordering on uncomfortable.

"I'm not going to bother you out here on the field while you're working, am I?" he asks.

"Nope, not at all. In fact, my brother sometimes comes out to watch with me. He might come tonight, so he can keep you company if I get too busy."

"Which brother?"

I can't help but laugh at the way he asked. "Jonathan. Simon's usually on his shift until about midnight."

"It would be great to see him while I'm in town."

And right there is the reminder that Conner is leaving soon. This time next week, he will be gone and out of my life again. I can't help but wonder if he intends to not keep in touch again. That this visit was a little trip down memory lane for him . . . not realizing that memory lane for me has been slightly more stressful than it should be.

"He might, it depends if he can get out of the office early enough." Then I remember who else is coming tonight. "Oh, yeah, I almost forgot. My boss, Dylan, is probably going to show up at some point, if he's not already here."

I'm pretty sure I sounded like a pretty poor liar when I tried to play it off that Dylan is *just* my boss. But it's not like I can tell Conner he's more than that since I don't even know what he is to me anymore.

"Well, don't let me get in the way. Pretend I'm not here, Shadow."

Pretending that he isn't here will be impossible, but I do get back to work. I do this just in time to catch the Barracudas score a touchdown and then a two-point conversion immediately afterward. As I'm taking a picture of the team's celebration, I hear a familiar and not welcome voice coming from behind me.

"I haven't been to a high school football game since high school, Dylan."

He brought Rachel.

The crushing feeling I get knowing that he brought Rachel here is enough for me to see red. Making it impossible for me to turn around and say hello or just acknowledge him. Because Dylan knows how much all of this means to me. He knows that this is what I live for. And yet, he brought her here. Which makes me then think that he's trying to prove a point. But what that point is, I haven't the faintest idea.

"Should we say hello?"

Rachel, who I guess must be wondering why they haven't announced themselves to me yet, asks this. Because I'm sure she's dying to rub it in my face that she has Dylan all to herself.

I can't make out what he says back to her. But whatever it was, they still don't come over to me. Should I bite the bullet and get it over with? If I do, it will be difficult to hide how much I dislike the idea of her being here. But maybe that's a good thing for him to see.

So I put down my camera, letting it hang around my neck as I turn around to find them. Dylan was already looking straight at me before I start walking to him . . . them. He keeps his eyes trained on me as Rachel's attention is momentarily diverted to the cheerleaders. It's not a long walk, but it feels like it takes forever and a day to reach them.

Just then, Rachel starts to talk about how she was a cheerleader in high school since she's not paying any mind to either of us. So we stand awkwardly there, looking at each other. I want to say so many things to him, but I can't narrow it down to only one. You would think that saying hello to someone you've seen almost every day for the past six or seven years would be much easier than this.

But then Rachel turns around excitedly to say something else about the cheerleaders to Dylan and notices me standing there, still as a statue.

"Oh, Katy, there you are."

I tear my eyes away from him and smile at Rachel. "Yup, here I am. I was . . . am working."

"Doesn't this get boring?" she says with a fake yawn. "When I was in high school, my friends and I would be bored out of our minds on the sidelines."

Dylan rubs the back of his head, obviously not wanting to touch her comment with a ten-foot pole. My blood boils and I want to say so many things back to her, but I'm having a hard time just juggling work and my personal life at the same time.

"It's not boring to me," I finally tell her. "As a matter of fact, I—"

Right then, Conner sidles up to me and says, "Barracudas are about to take the lead, Katy."

But even that fact doesn't tear me away from the look in Dylan's eyes as he takes in Conner for the first time. It's enough to make me more uncomfortable than I already am. It's not outright jealousy I see in his eyes, but confusion is also there in the way his eyebrows scrunch together a little.

I decide to at least be civil and introduce everyone to each other. "Conner, this is my boss, Dylan." Conner offers his hand to shake Dylan's. "Dylan, this is my old friend Conner I was telling you about."

"It's nice to meet you," Conner says and Dylan nods. Then he looks to Rachel, noticing her just standing there, and I realize that I didn't even bother with her introduction.

"I'm Rachel, by the way," she says and offers her hand for Conner to shake. She looks to me with a sideways glance and then says in a not-so-quiet voice, "I didn't know you had a boyfriend, Katy. You should have said something, we could all have gone out on a double date."

My stomach drops to somewhere around my knees while Conner laughs it off. But he throws his arm around my shoulders and pulls me closer to him. I glance up and catch his eyes with a bit of a twinkle of mischief in them as he says, "We're just old friends."

Rachel nudges Dylan's ribs and says, "Don't they look cute together? Why don't we invite them to go for a drink after the game or something?"

He leans in and whispers something in her ear. When he does this her hand affectionately rests on his chest until he's done talking. My mind goes to a couple of days ago when I was that close to him, and the thought brings a feeling of helplessness over me. Because this is it, I think. It can't be more obvious than the way they are so comfortable with each other . . . sharing a secret like two lovers who are oblivious to anyone around them.

Rachel snorts a laugh, which snaps me back to the here and now. I'm so startled by that sound coming from her that I can't help but laugh. Dylan notices right away. He tries to hide his surprise by biting his lip, and Conner . . . well, he's just along for the ride.

His arm is still around my shoulders when Jonathan comes walking up behind Dylan and Rachel. I have never been so happy to see one of my brothers in my entire life. I would have taken Simon's appearance at this point in the festivities, that's how much I need a reprieve.

"Excuse me," I say quickly and dart out from Conner's hold. In an almost sprint, I reach my brother. "Thank God you're here."

"Is that Conner?" he asks, looking over my shoulder. "And Dylan?"

"Yes and yes."

"Who's that?" He points to Rachel with a look of confusion. "Is that the infamous Rachel?"

I nod, hoping that the sheer panic on my face is enough to encapsulate the level of stress I am currently in.

"And here I was thinking it would be a nice, relaxing Friday night," he says and winks at me. "You owe me."

"Thank you, thank you, thank you!" I reach up and give him a big hug. "Lunch is on me for the next month if you can distract everyone."

"Katy, I'm a lawyer, not a magician," he says. "Okay, here goes nothing."

CHAPTER NINETEEN

Whatever hidden talents as a magician Jonathan has seem to work, because the rest of the time at the game goes by much more smoothly and definitely less uncomfortably. I can't guess as to what is running through Dylan's mind, but the tension is defused by at least ten or so notches. Which lets me get back to doing my job, which is what I am here for in the first place.

By the time the game is over and I'm sitting on one of the sideline benches as usual, outlining my article, I hope that Dylan and Rachel have left so I don't have to experience an awkward good-bye. But much to my chagrin, I close my iPad and look over to find all of them, Jonathan included, still milling around on the far side of the field, closer to the exit gates.

I look up to the heavens and say quietly, "Can't I catch a break?"

It's not like I can sit here by myself and pretend nobody else is here, because at this point in the night, they are pretty much the only people on the field. Everyone else is either hanging out in the parking lot or has already left. Standing up as if the weight of the world is on my shoulders, I tuck my iPad and camera into my messenger bag. Then I throw the strap over my head before walking toward them as if I had cement blocks tied to my feet.

"Shadow, we were just talking about you."

"Really? What about?" I ask.

"Shadow?" Dylan asks at the same time.

Then Jonathan chimes in. "Wow, I haven't heard that nickname in years."

"Who is Shadow?" Rachel asks. Conner and Jonathan point to me. She then asks, "What kind of nickname is that for a girl?"

"She used to follow me around like she was my shadow from the first day we met," Conner explains with a knowing smile. "The name stuck."

I notice Dylan's eyes flick to Conner, then to me, the tension coming back into the conversation again. Jonathan, thankfully, saves me.

"All right, so, Conner . . . it was great seeing you again, man. Have a safe trip back home if I don't catch you before you leave. And I'll make sure to let Simon know you said hello and you were sorry you missed him this time around."

He says this and does one of those man-bro hug things with Conner, who is trying hard not to laugh. Seriously, Simon isn't all that bad. But I can't blame Conner for not wanting to go back down that road.

"Great seeing you too," he says to Jonathan. Then, standing up straight, he puts out his hand to Dylan. "It was nice meeting you, Dylan, and you, Rachel."

"Are you guys leaving?" Dylan asks, looking right at me.

Conner's attention turns to me. "What do you think, Shadow?"

"Sure, I'm ready."

"Are you ready to go, Dylan?" Rachel asks. "We can go back to my place and try that wine I was telling you about."

You can hear a pin drop waiting for someone else to speak up. But out of all of us, it's Jonathan who decides to say something. "All right, well, I'll catch up with you tomorrow, Katy." He looks around to everyone and then says good night before leaving.

"Come on, Katy," Conner says. "I bet you haven't even eaten yet. I've got some food I can throw on the grill back at my house."

My vision is clouded with jealousy when I answer, looking straight at Dylan. "That sounds great. Let's go."

If it bothers him, he doesn't let on. He politely puts his hand on Rachel's back and says good night to Conner and me. Rachel follows suit, throwing over her shoulder an overenthusiastic good night, then lets Dylan guide her to the parking lot.

"So, are you ready?" Conner asks. I nod and he motions his hand with a flourish over to the almost empty parking lot. "After you, Shadow."

I'm walking slightly ahead of Conner, but my eyes track Dylan and Rachel as they disappear into his car and drive away. And when I finally get into mine to drive to Conner's house, all I can think about is Dylan and how I must have missed the signs from day one.

CHAPTER TWENTY

Seven years ago . . .

I was so nervous.

I'd been preparing for this interview all night until I fell asleep with my face on my desk. I woke up to my blaring alarm clock and the yelling of my not-so-understanding college roommate, Natasha.

Now, as I sat there waiting to meet the editor in chief of the college newspaper, I doubted myself. I had heard stories about him through the campus grapevine. In my journalism class, he was the topic of conversation almost every day. There were a few of us in that class who were vying for the few open slots this year, and the consensus was that Dylan Sterling could spot talent a mile away. So naturally, we each thought we would be the one he would pick.

I had always thought I could spend my life as a sports journalist. But at that very moment, staring at the wood door that said "Editor in Chief," I didn't feel ready. There was no way that a lowly freshman would be considered for a spot that would normally go to a senior . . . and usually one of the opposite sex. But I had to try.

As I toyed with the hem of my collared shirt, I thought for a split second about leaving. Maybe I should just come back next year after a new editor in chief was in place. Since Dylan Sterling was a senior, he would be long gone and I wouldn't have to bear the weight of his rejection. Which I'd been told could be brutal. I was just getting ready to scurry out of there when his door creaked open and a very handsome man with bright green eyes looked at me and asked, "Katy Lewis?"

"Yes," I croaked and then cleared my throat. "That's me."

I held out my hand for a handshake. He reciprocated with a puzzled look. I thought, this is it . . . *he knows I'm not good enough and already has a preconceived notion about women reporting on sports. I should have left when I had the chance.*

"Please, come into my office." He opened the door wider for me to walk past him.

His office was small and sparsely decorated. An open laptop sat on a utilitarian desk, and there were papers strewn about in some sort of organized chaos. On top of one pile of papers was a pair of black Ray-Ban eyeglasses. And on another pile was a framed picture of Dylan with a very beautiful girl in his arms.

I could tell the woman in the photograph was his match in every possible way. They looked good together, and I stamped down a very fleeting stab of jealousy. It's not like he would be interested in someone like me . . . plain and mousy. Of course he would be with someone like her: long dark hair, piercing green eyes, and a gorgeous smile. She looked as if she had just finished running some sort of road race since a number was tagged to her tank top. Well, obviously he would be hugging her if she ran a marathon . . . she's perfect, for God's sake.

"You two make a beautiful couple," I said, pointing at the picture.

Dylan, who was in the middle of sitting down, froze. And then he smiled and asked, "What makes you think we're a couple?"

"Well, I just assumed," I said, fumbling. "You both look very happy and you're both very good-looking and . . . I don't know." My cheeks felt as if they were on fire, because not only had I started this interview totally wrong, I'd just told him I thought he was good-looking.

He chuckled. "That's my sister, Carrie, but thank you for all those nice things you said about her . . . and me."

"Oh God," I said under my breath. "I'm so sorry." I started to gather my things and stood up to leave.

"Wait a second, where are you going? The interview hasn't even started yet."

Plopping down in my seat again in defeat, I said, "I'm really sorry. I got about an hour's worth of sleep last night prepping for this interview and don't know what I'm saying and probably shouldn't be talking anymore since I keep sticking my foot in my mouth."

Dylan leaned forward, resting his elbows on his desk. "Ms. Lewis, there is no reason to be nervous. Take a deep breath and relax."

I just sat there and stared at him, at those eyes . . . they were mesmerizing.

"Go ahead, do it," he said. "I promise, it will make you feel better and we can move on to why you're really here."

So I took a breath, held it, and then exhaled.

"One more time," Dylan encouraged with a knowing smile.

Once I blew out that last breath, I did feel a tiny bit better.

"Are you ready then, Ms. Lewis?" he asked.

I nodded. "You don't have to call me that. My name is Katy."

"Well then, Katy," he said. "Which position are you here for?"

"Sports beat."

I handed him my portfolio, and to his credit, he didn't laugh or pause with that look I usually get from men when they hear what type of news I want to cover. It's a look that's a mix of incredulousness and amusement. But Dylan Sterling simply took the articles I had been carefully clipping and saving from my high school paper for the past couple of years, then placed them on his desk and started going through them. I watched nervously as he reached for his glasses and put them on, adjusting them once in a while as he read.

It was so quiet you could hear a pin drop. Every so often, I would catch him peering up at me over the top rim of his eyeglasses, and I would quickly look away. I could swear that with every sneaking glance, Dylan was trying to figure me out. And not in a patronizing way either. It was as if he knew already that I was capable enough. That he wasn't the least bit surprised that I was a good journalist on my way to being an even better one.

When he finished reading, he closed the portfolio and didn't say a word for a beat, but it felt more like an eternity. He studied me openly. Dylan stared at me and so I stared back. I didn't know whether he was trying to intimidate me or if he was trying to figure out a way to gently tell me that I didn't get the job.

His stare continued until finally I broke under the pressure and looked away again. If anything, I was sure that Dylan Sterling was the king of the stare down. I'd heard he could be a bit intimidating and a lot formidable. But face-to-face, he had an air about him that made you comfortable, regardless of his obvious staring problem.

But the most consistent rumor about him was that he didn't mix business with pleasure. Dylan Sterling never even dated anyone who was a journalism major. I laughed to myself as I sat there. I didn't know why I thought it was so comical, but I did.

"Is something funny?" he asked as I tried pathetically to cover my mouth and stop snickering.

"No, not at all, I'm sorry, I just was thinking that . . ." Then I thought better of it. "You know what, never mind. It's not important."

"Please, go ahead." Dylan actually looked entertained, but I was horrified.

"Well," I started. "Well, it's silly, really. But there is a rumor that you don't date anyone who works at the newspaper or who is a journalism major."

His face morphed into a kind smile. "And this bothers you?"

"Oh my God, no! Nothing like that! I was just—"

"You were just wondering if it were true?"

He still didn't seem put off by my question or how this interview was a disaster from the start. Dylan's eyes grazed over me in the quiet that suddenly consumed the room, but it didn't feel lecherous or wrong. Instead, he looked at me as if I was his equal and—dare I say—pretty? No, that wasn't it, was it? Maybe a little bit. It made my skin flush with excitement to think that perhaps he thought of me in that way.

Then I snapped out of that delusion as quickly as it appeared in my thoughts when he cleared his throat and said, "It's not true, I just haven't met the right girl."

"Oh."

And I didn't risk saying another word for fear that I would tank this interview more than I already had.

"Ms. Lewis," he then said and took off his eyeglasses. "I—"

"It's Katy," I interrupted him and smiled stiffly, knowing that he was about to dismiss me.

"Right, sorry, Katy." He handed me the portfolio with the best poker face I'd ever seen. "Your writing is strong and you demonstrate great insight in your pieces. I'm sure your high school paper was sad to see you go."

I thanked him with a shrug of my shoulders and braced myself for the rejection. But it didn't come.

"Katy," he then said with a grin. "I think this is the beginning of a beautiful friendship."

CHAPTER TWENTY-ONE

T hat was delicious. Thank you, Conner."

"You're welcome."

The burger he grilled was to die for. I must have eaten it in about four or five bites, that's how good it was.

"I didn't know you could cook," I say after wiping my mouth with a napkin. "If I did, I would have been over here every night this week."

His back is to me while he scrubs the grill clean. "Every night, huh?"

"Yup."

"Then maybe I should have told you before that I could cook."

I wish I could see his face when he says this, because his voice is so serious that I'm not sure if he's joking. He closes the top of the grill and wipes his hands on a towel that was thrown over his shoulder, then finally turns around. That sly smile of his is back in place and that usual warm feeling I get when I see it instantly makes me nervous. Because here we are, all alone, it's almost pitch-dark, if not for the light coming from the pool illuminating the backyard. I look inside myself, trying to find something light and easy to say, but nothing comes out. So I just sit there looking like an idiot, waiting for the other shoe to drop.

Conner goes to open the cooler and asks if I want another beer. I decline, saying that I have to drive home and one was good enough for me. Then he drags a chair over and plants it right next to me, sitting down and leaning as far back as he can. I watch from the corner of my eye as he stretches his arms over his head, revealing a tiny bit of the tan skin of his taut stomach. A flush comes over me and I look away quickly, not wanting to be caught red-handed. He finally gets settled and pops open his beer, taking a long sip before holding it loosely in his hand between us.

"It's a nice night, right?" I ask and then fidget in my seat. "A little hot, though, for late September."

"Why don't you take off your sweatshirt then?"

My head spins to him and my eyes go wide in disbelief. "What?"

"You just said it was hot, but you're wearing a sweatshirt, yes?"

"Yeah, but I can't take it off."

He was in the middle of bringing the beer bottle to his lips and freezes. He glances down to my sweatshirt or chest and then up to my face with a knowing smile. "I can lend you a T-shirt if you want."

"No, no, it's fine. I'll be fine," I say too quickly. Sounding nervous and anxious and feeling as if I might melt from not only the heat of the night but the heat I'm pretty sure I saw in Conner's eyes as he was inspecting my clothes.

"We can go for a dip in the pool."

"Conner, if I didn't know you any better, I'd say you were trying to get me naked."

The word naked and Conner's name in the same sentence were not the right choice, and I instantly regret it. Because all I can see in my head now is visions of him naked, me naked, us naked . . . just lots and lots of naked. Too much naked for me to process or handle right now.

Covering my face with my hands, I say, "Pretend I didn't say that, okay?"

"Sure," he says, chuckling. "It's like it never happened."

Something about the way he says that reminds me about the letter and the fact that we haven't spoken a thing about it. It *is* like it never happened. Like all of this is just making up for lost time and that I'm supposed to act a certain way with him but I don't know how. And Conner doesn't seem fazed at all by any of it.

That's when I start to go from embarrassed to angry. No, angry isn't quite the right word to describe how I've felt ever since he showed back up in my life a week ago. Confused is more like it. And as much as I don't want to revisit that specific part of my past, I can't go on being around him without addressing it. It's too heavy of a weight on my shoulders. Either we're going to be friends and fix things between us or we move on our separate ways and call this for what it is: two friends playing catch-up.

Channeling the anger from years past to this moment, I somehow put it aside and muster the courage I need to move forward.

"Conner, I need to ask you something."

He senses the seriousness in my voice and leans forward in his seat without saying a word, letting the beer bottle dangle in between his fingers.

I keep my eyes trained on the bottle as it catches the light before finally getting my lips to move. "I was so hurt when I lashed out at you that night, but I never expected you to totally disappear on me either. I mean, you never wrote or called . . . nothing. You were just gone. It was like one moment you were in every part of my life and the next you weren't. It was as if our friendship meant nothing to you, Conner."

Still staring at the beer bottle in his hand, I breathe a little easier having put it all out there in the open. But his silence is deafening. Until he puts the bottle down quietly on the ground and stands up. Then he crouches in front of me, putting his hands on the armrests of my chair. I instantly sit back to try to put some space between us, but where can I go? I'm in a chair and he's *right* there . . . I'm trapped.

"Shadow," he says softly. "Look at me."

Without picking up my head, I do as he asks, letting my eyes roam to his for a fleeting glance before concentrating really hard on the ground again.

Conner gently puts his hand underneath my chin, lifting my face up to meet his.

"There you are," he says. He takes a quick breath. "Do you know how long I've wanted to talk about this? About that night? About that letter?"

"Why didn't you?" The emotion in my voice is almost strangling me. I can't help the knee-jerk reaction and the consequent tears that build up in my eyes until one lone tear leaks out and falls down my cheek.

"Please don't cry, Katy," he says. "I can take a lot of things, but seeing you cry was never one of them."

"I'm a girl, we cry sometimes," I say and he smiles faintly.

"That night wasn't the first time I knew things were different between us," he says after a long pause. "I knew how you felt about me, and I would be a liar if I didn't admit that I felt something for you too. But doing something about it is totally different. I didn't want to lose you as my friend."

"But you did anyway. You left and never looked back. Do you know how hard that night was for me? Do you have any idea how much you hurt me by taking away your friendship, Conner?"

"I do."

"Then why?"

"Because I had to, Shadow. Because if I didn't, then I would have been stringing you along while you were here and I was across the country. Because we were kids and I was terrified at the prospect of things changing between us." He moves an inch or two closer to me, his face hovering over mine, and he is all I can see. Those hazel eyes boring into mine, looking for something that he lost in the hopes of finding it tonight. Then, oh so quietly, he whispers, "Do you know how many times I've regretted doing that to you? I can't begin to tell you the many nights I picked up the phone to call you. Or all the times I started to write you a letter and never got past the 'Dear Katy' part." Conner pauses, moving even closer. His takes my face gently in his hands, running his thumbs across my cheeks softly. "Do you know how hard it is for me to be around you again? Do you know that every time I've seen you in the last week I've wanted to take you in my arms and beg for your forgiveness?"

I wrap my hands around his wrists. My heart thumping away in my chest as the moment I've been waiting for is within my grasp.

"That letter, Katy, it was too much too fast that night. I couldn't, no matter how much I wanted you in that way. It would have been wrong, and you know it just as much as I do. Did you actually think I thought so little of you that I could take that from you in my backseat that same night?"

I shake my head, feeling a little confused and a lot overwhelmed by everything he's saying.

Then in an almost whisper, he asks, "Do you know how much I want to kiss you, Katy?"

Without another word, he tilts my head a fraction, leaning in the rest of the tiny space left between us. And when I close my eyes, he presses his lips to mine finally.

At first it's a soft brush of his mouth against mine, and my mind goes blank just luxuriating in the moment. Then he angles my head just so to be able to feast on my lips. And when his tongue darts out slowly to touch mine, I lose myself completely. It's as if I'm floating on a cloud and I never want to come down.

Until the last thing I ever expected comes popping into my head: Dylan.

I pull away from Conner's kiss. Sitting back in my chair, getting some much needed air in my lungs. I feel as if I might as well have thrown a bucket of ice-cold water over my head. Because the cloud I had been floating on comes crashing to the ground. And all I can see in my mind's eye is Dylan with Rachel and just how much I don't want that to happen. I actually don't want that to happen more than I want *this* to happen with Conner.

"Katy?"

I can't find the words to explain myself. I'm sweating and I'm not sure if it's from the kiss, the night's humidity, or because I'm losing my mind.

"Is everything all right? Should I not have done that?"

Conner searches my face for the answer. But my head is still reeling from a revelation that is bouncing around and taking hold of my heart in its grubby little paws: I think I am in love with Dylan.

Immediately followed by: I need to get out of here before I make the biggest mistake of my life.

CHAPTER TWENTY-TWO

Overwhelmed, I need to pull over to the side of the road after leaving Conner's house. It's when I'm parked on that side street that I break down and really lose it.

How stupid am I for letting this . . . *all* of this . . . get as far as it has? Not only with Dylan, but also with Conner. I should have known better than to bring up the letter. I should have left things as they were. He's leaving next week and he could have gone on his merry way without a thing being said or that kiss happening, which could have led to who knows what.

And oh God, the look on Conner's face when I told him I had to leave was one I'll never forget. I start to laugh a little maniacally at this because it must be the same look I had on my face when I left him in Bayview Park almost nine years ago.

So I sit here and think. And think. And think some more. Trying to plan out my next move like a game of chess. Then in slow motion, my hand darts out and reaches for my cell phone.

As if on autopilot, I text Dylan, hoping that he'll answer. Not noticing until after I press Send that it's almost midnight and he could very well be sleeping. Or worse, tied up with Rachel.

Are you home?

I stare at our text exchange, looking for the telltale three running dots that indicate he's typing something back.

They don't come.

I chuck the phone onto my passenger seat and rest my head against the steering wheel in defeat. Because what was I going to do if he said yes?

But right then, my phone vibrates and I snatch it up to see his response.

Yes. Are you?

Quickly, I text back:

No. Are you alone?

The three dots string together until I see his answer.

Yes.

I smile as a tear rolls down my cheek in relief. But it's not enough, I need to see him in person and hope that he doesn't think I'm absolutely crazy for asking.

Can I come over?

It takes more than a minute for him to answer. I know this because I stare at the phone the whole time, and when it starts dimming before it auto-locks, I touch the screen to bring it back to life.

Then finally, his answer comes and it terrifies me and thrills me all at the same time.

Yes.

———

I get to Dylan's condo in about ten minutes. I wasn't racing, but I definitely wasn't doing the speed limit either. And it's times like these I remember that my brother's a cop and could probably get me out of the ticket. I've never ever used that crutch, and never would under any other circumstances, but today is different.

Today, right now, is something I never saw myself doing.

If someone had told me last week that I'd reject Conner in any scenario, I probably would have said they were on drugs. But more than that, if someone would have told me I was in love with Dylan and would be on my way to his house in the middle of the night, I'd tell them they should be committed.

But here I am. No turning back now.

And I don't want to. I need to see him like I need to take my next breath to survive.

I park my car and leave everything in it, only taking my keys, which I throw into the pocket of my hoodie sweatshirt. With each step away from my car and to Dylan's door, a weight slowly lifts from my shoulders.

I reach up to knock on his front door but it swings open. Dylan is standing on the other side without his eyeglasses, propping the door open with his arm and wearing nothing but drawstring pajama bottoms that hang low on his hips, leaving nothing to the imagination. His long, sleek, and muscular torso is on full display, and my first instinct is to reach out and run my hands across all that skin. A thrill runs through me as my eyes canvass his strong jaw, his neck and shoulders, and the smattering of hair on his tan chest that runs down and disappears into his pajama bottoms. But I hesitate, because there is a storm brewing in his normally brilliant eyes.

We stand there for a few seconds not talking or moving. I'm barely breathing and afraid I made a monumental mistake in coming here, so I take a step back to leave, second-guessing myself. Dylan grabs my arm, pulling me inside. Then he slams the door behind me and takes a couple of steps forward until my back is pinned against it. It takes me a moment to gather my wits, but when I do, I'm hyperaware of his body pressed against mine.

His hands bracket me against the door. "What do you want, Katy?"

I can't answer right away because I want so many things at that moment, but in the end it's just him. He's what I want. But I don't know how to tell him that, so the words get lodged somewhere in my throat.

His jaw ticks in frustration at my silence, and he leans his head in closer and closer, until his cheek runs alongside mine. The day old stubble rasps against my skin and brings a thrill up my spine. Then, when he reaches my ear, he whispers again, "What do you want?"

When I don't answer, he asks just as quietly, "Why aren't you with him?"

"I don't know." My heart twists with the lie since I know that I want to be here with Dylan. Be consumed by him.

"Did you let him touch you?" he asks after searching my eyes, my lips, my soul.

"Yes, but I could only think about you," I say. "Did you touch her?"

He shakes his head slowly, bringing a relief so great to my heart and mind that I blow out a long breath. He asks, "Does that bother you? The idea of Rachel and me together?"

"Yes," I admit quietly.

"Why?"

"Because I didn't know until recently how you felt . . . how much *I* felt. I've been so confused since I left your office the other day and I didn't know how to act around you. But then I saw you with her tonight . . . it bothered me. I wanted to be the one at your side, Dylan."

Then he brings one of his hands to cup the side of my face. He drags his cheek along mine again until his lips are but a breath away from mine, his eyes now pinning me to him. "Did he kiss you?"

I nod, not wanting to lie to him. If he's upset or disappointed in my answer, he doesn't let it show. He moves his other hand away from my head and slowly brings it underneath the hem of my sweatshirt, where his fingers lightly brush against my skin as they inch higher. When he touches the skin just below my breast, moving his fingers side to side, barely grazing me, my body comes alive and reacts immediately.

"Did he touch you here?"

"No," I answer, gasping for breath.

His hand moves higher until it's covering my breast, while his mouth presses a kiss on the corner of mine.

"Did he touch you here, Katy?"

My back arches off the door and into his warm touch. I shake my head, not able to string together a thought, much less a word right now.

"Do you want *me* to touch you?" he asks, moving his head back so that I can see clearly into his eyes. Looking back at me is pure, unadulterated lust on the cusp of being unleashed. And while his fingers now toy with the lace of my bra, he asks, "Do you want *me* to kiss you? Is that what you want?"

I nod again.

"Tell me. I need to hear you say it. I need to hear you ask me." He licks his lips, then says, "I'm afraid I won't be able to stop myself. I've wanted this . . . you. I've wanted *you* for so long."

Taking a gulp of much needed air, I answer him by pulling my sweatshirt over my head and tossing it to the ground behind him. The need for me to feel his bare skin against mine is overwhelming, so I reach behind me and unclasp my bra, sliding it down my arms as if it were on fire, until it hits the floor.

I bring my hands up to loop around his neck, luxuriating in the feel of our bare chests against each other's for the first time and look into his stormy eyes. "I want you, Dylan . . . I need you."

His hands rope around my back and he holds me to him tightly. Then, as if remembering I'm a real living and breathing thing in his arms, he pulls back slightly. His mouth is on mine before I can blink. The kiss is ravenous and full of hunger and amazing. Then, as if a switch trips in his head, his tongue plays with mine slowly and teasingly until I groan into his mouth, which spurs him on even more.

Dylan bends at the knees and hoists me up his body, wrapping my legs around his waist and walking us, I assume to his bedroom. But he stops and puts me down on his kitchen island. We're both breathing rapidly and it's as if we aren't sure where to even start with the other one.

I'm thirsty for more of him, so I run my fingers through his dark hair and trail my mouth along his jaw and down his throat. He tastes indescribably delicious: like a summer's day melting against my tongue. He moans my name out loud, and it nearly destroys me. Because the way he says it is like a prayer that has been finally answered.

He then takes my ponytail and wraps it around his hand. Yanking it lightly down to expose my throat, he ducks his head and starts to kiss a trail to my breasts. The farther he gets, the farther my body slides down the island until I'm lying on my back completely.

He laves my breasts with long swipes of his tongue, gently sucking on my nipples, taking turns with each one as I grip his hair and try to pull him closer to me. Then Dylan looks up at me as my nipple pops out of his mouth and is about to say something, but I put my finger to his mouth to keep him from talking.

"Don't stop. Please," I say, squirming underneath him.

He reaches for the button and zipper of my jeans, undoing them deftly, and quickly pulls them down my legs just after I kick off my sneakers. Leaving me in my underwear, he drapes his body completely over mine. He's kissing me for all he's worth and pressing his hardness against where I need it most. I don't know where to put my hands or my mouth, because I want them everywhere all at once. And by the way he touches, kisses, licks, and nips at me, I know he's having the same problem.

But then he's on the move again, going down my body, using his mouth as his compass until he reaches the lacey trim of my panties. He looks up at me as his thumbs hook underneath on either side of them, slowly peeling them off of me. Then, without any fanfare, he's placing my feet on the island and spreading my thighs with his hands. His vibrant green eyes are staring up at me when he takes his first taste of me; a long, teasing lick up and then down my center. It's enough to make my eyes roll into the back of my head. And before long, with his tongue and hands working my body in unison, he's bringing me to climax and I'm shouting his name out loud.

As I'm coming down, my body already knows it wants more from him. I need to have him inside me . . . it's like a life-or-death situation. So I sit up and kiss him, tasting the remnants of myself on his tongue, which turns me on even more. I reach down in between us and slide my hand inside his pajama bottoms. Taking him in my grip, I move up and down while watching his expression turn to one of ecstasy. It's beautiful . . . *he's* beautiful.

Dylan rests a hand on the middle of my chest and pushes me until I'm lying flat on my back. Slowly he pulls his bottoms off and is standing before me completely naked for the first time. He's perfect . . . everywhere. From the finely sculpted muscles of his chest, to the line of his hipbone, and finally to the happy trail that leads to where he's slowly stroking himself.

He leans over me, bracing one arm on the side of my head while rubbing his hardness across where I'm still very sensitive . . . once, twice, three times. Then he stills at my entrance. And with one strong stroke, he pushes inside of me.

The feeling of wanting him to move is so great that I pull my legs up higher and wrap them tighter around his waist. He slides out of me slowly, and then pushes back in hard and fast. I grip his shoulders for leverage, trying to hold on to him and this moment for much longer than it will last.

Dylan groans into my neck and slides his hand down my throat until it rests on my breast, where he plucks at my nipple with his thumb and forefinger. The sensation ricochets to my core, where his rhythm is now at a perfect pace, sensual and smooth. And then he rams into me so hard that my back bows off of the kitchen island in pure bliss.

Within seconds, with each powerful and calculated thrust of Dylan's, I'm on the brink again. Wanting so badly to fall over that cliff but not wanting it to end at the same time. He suddenly picks his head up to look down at me underneath him. As if for the first time he's realizing that it's really me—Katy, *his* Katy—that he's inside of and bringing to climax for the second time tonight. He freezes all of his movements and cups my face with his hand. Tenderly, he presses his lips to mine, kissing me like he has all the time in the world and the night will never end.

While his tongue dances with mine, he starts to move again. In and out, faster and harder, building us both up until neither of us can keep up with the kiss that has slowly unraveled into this mesh of bodies and sweat and hands gripping on to each other and my nails scraping down his back. And that's when my body pulls at him, climaxing around him, making him rear his head back and groan loudly as he finally reaches his peak.

My legs, now weak and tired, fall to the sides. Dylan collapses on top of me, my body welcoming his warmth like it was a blanket on a cold winter's day. Our breathing slowly returns to normal as we lie in each other's arms for what feels like an eternity. Reality slowly worms its way into my head . . . worrying that it will never be better than this moment right here with him.

Knowing me too well, I think he senses my mind is already racing, so he presses a soft kiss on my neck and I instantly relax. His lips slowly trace my jaw and move to my mouth, where he brushes his lips against mine and breathes into me, bringing me back to life for him and for the rest of the night and wherever this will take us.

When Dylan lifts me up and carries me into his bedroom, still inside of me, still hard and my body welcoming his still, he only says a few words about not letting me sleep tonight before he lays me down and starts to move again. This time our lovemaking is excruciatingly slow and almost calculated . . . but it's exactly what I need and want.

And after we eventually climax together again, he stays inside of me, rolling me over until I'm on top of him. His eyes dance across my face, my body, and in my heart. When he's pulling me close so I can lie on him and rest, he runs his hand through my hair, my ponytail long gone.

Dylan lets the strands run through his fingers again and again.

"Don't go," he says into the darkness.

I nod into his chest, smiling as my eyes grow heavy and I succumb to a peaceful and dreamless sleep in his arms.

CHAPTER TWENTY-THREE

In the light of day usually everything looks better. Or worse, depending on how much of a pessimist you truly are.

For me, the light of this new day brings a vivid reminder of what I did last night.

I literally put the wheels in motion and had mind-blowing sex with Dylan, who has been one of my best friends for years. If that wasn't enough for a one-in-a-million evening, I rejected Conner, who was my best friend growing up. I kind of left him hanging last night and I can only imagine what is running through his mind right now.

When my eyes slowly adjust to the light in Dylan's bedroom, I look to my left to find him still asleep like a baby. He's lying on his stomach with an arm thrown over his head on the pillow. His dark hair is seriously bed-sex tousled and his lips are parted just enough that they are completely kissable. An urge so deep to do just that comes over me as I study the slope of his upper lip and how the bottom lip almost pouts as he sleeps. But I don't.

The biggest thing that happened last night, apart from the obvious, was that I realized I could be in love with Dylan. And here's the tricky part: when I separate my body from the equation, is that really true? Or is it just because I saw him with Rachel?

I can't think clearly about any of this while Dylan is lying next to me naked underneath the blanket, which is barely covering his backside. So I look up to the ceiling, trying to relax, only to find myself getting more and more worked up with anxiety that I might have made a terrible mistake.

The light of day sucks.

I slowly peel away the blanket and slide out of bed as smoothly as possible, trying my hardest not to make a sound and to be as quiet as a church mouse. Dylan doesn't stir or open his eyes, thank God. I tiptoe out of his room and down his hallway, making my way to the kitchen to pick up and put on some of my clothes. Then I head to the entryway to pick up and put on the rest of my clothes. I make an executive decision not to put my sneakers back on until I'm safely outside, for fear that they might make a squeaking noise against the hardwood floor.

My hand freezes on his doorknob; the only sound I can hear is the soft hissing of the air conditioner and then nothing . . . nothing but the steady thrum of my heart beating, building and building with each step I take closer to the door.

Leaving Dylan feels as sneaky and dirty as it looks to the outside eye, like a thief running off into the night. But in my case, it's the early morning hours after the best night of my life. I decide right then and there to go home and take some "me time" to figure out what I'm going to do next and push away the nagging thought that I'm making yet another mistake.

Closing the door with the stealth of a well-trained burglar, I speed walk to my car in the parking lot. Once I'm safely inside, I grab my phone and see five missed calls from Simon, two from Conner, and one text from Mimi, which says:

Wherever you are and whoever you're with, I hope it's worth it because Simon is looking for you and driving me nuts. xo

Oh no, I didn't even think to let Mimi know that I wasn't coming home last night. Knowing her, she probably got Simon off her back eventually, but I'm sure it took a while. I'll just swing by Starbucks and pick her up a coffee and something sweet for breakfast to make it up to her. And then figure out how to deal with Simon later, because there are more important things to concern myself with right now.

I spare one last glance at Dylan's door as I'm putting my car in drive and ignore the ache in my chest when I pull out of the parking lot and onto the street to go home.

———

When I arrive at the apartment with two cups of Starbucks and a baggie of goodies for Mimi and me, it's still really early. Obscenely early . . . so early that the beach traffic that usually builds up in and around the Fort Lauderdale area is not yet to be seen.

I decide to talk things out with Mimi. Hopefully she's awake and willing to listen without too much interruption and commentary and, God bless her, analogies to movies that make no sense whatsoever in relation to my life.

With a little juggling, I'm able to hold the coffee tray and unlock the front door, only to walk in on the most disturbing scene I've ever been witness to.

Simon is behind Mimi, gripping her hips. She's bent over and holding on to the back of the couch with her back to him, and he's got his pants off, and thankfully Mimi's body is covering *that* part. But she's covering *that* part of his body because he's plowing into her like there is no tomorrow.

Now, I've seen Mimi semi-naked before. But never *this* much naked. Because the amount of naked I'm getting an eyeful of right now is just not normal to share with friends. Like, ever.

"Holy shit!"

I yell this at the top of my lungs and drop the coffee tray on the floor, followed by the bag of goodies. Then my hands fly up to cover my eyes since I'm pretty sure they feel like they've been doused in acid.

Turning around like I was getting ready to play pin the tail on the donkey, I hear rustling of clothes and cursing coming from both Simon and Mimi. With my back turned to them, I reach out blindly with one hand, eyes tightly shut still, and slam the door so loud I'm pretty sure that if the neighbors weren't awake after me yelling, they're definitely awake now.

"Are you dressed?!" I ask, still yelling.

"Hang on, hang on," Mimi says as I hear her or both of them rushing around behind me. "Okay, you can turn around."

Slowly I turn around and open my eyes. Simon is still straightening his uniform and Mimi is sitting on the couch in her robe, twirling a piece of her hair between her fingers and looking everywhere but me.

"Where the hell have you been? I've been worried sick about you," Simon says. "Did you even think to check your cell phone, Katy? Or call me back or something so I wouldn't be here looking for you at all hours of the night?"

My mouth drops open, and nothing, not a word or the slightest sound, comes out. Because he has got to be kidding me right now.

I look to Mimi, who is rolling her eyes at Simon and then finally gets the nerve to glance in my direction. She notices the spilled Starbucks coffee cups on the ground and says, "Oooh, was that for me? I could really use one right about now."

"You could really use one right about now?" I repeat in shock.

They look at each other, and Simon at least has the decency to look halfway embarrassed. Mimi, on the other hand, looks as if it's just another day at the office. And then it clicks . . .

I point to Simon while talking to her. "It's him? Simon is your mystery guy? And don't you dare lie to me or I swear I won't tell you anything about my personal life again."

"Did something new happen last night?" she asks and clasps her hands together in excitement. "Oh my God, did you sleep with Conner or Dylan? Tell me everything and don't you dare hold out on me! I'm dying to know!"

Simon starts to yell at the top of his lungs, "What the hell is she talking about, Katy? How many men are you involved with? And it better not be the Conner I remember, because that kid was an asshole!"

I love my brother to death, I really do. But the amount of times he has pulled his self-righteous and holier-than-thou attitude on me along with the usual overbearing nonsense has reached its limit. It ends today.

"Get out, Simon." I say this calmly and quietly.

"Not until you tell me where and who—"

Then I lose it. *"Get out!"*

It's so quiet you could hear a pin drop. Mimi then says, "She's not joking. You better get out of here, Simon."

He looks to Mimi and says, "I'll call you later."

Gathering up the last of his things, Simon storms by me and out the door, to which Mimi doesn't have any kind of reaction. Then she gets up and runs to the kitchen. She comes back to where I'm still standing, frozen in shock, and starts to clean up the spilled coffee.

Startling both of us out of the self-imposed silence is a loud knock on the door.

Mimi yells out, "Go home, Simon!"

But he ignores it and knocks even louder this time.

She curses under her breath and stands up, reaching for the door and swinging it open. It's not even halfway open when she starts to go off on him.

"Simon, for the love of God, just please—"

She cuts herself off and then says, "Oh, hey, Dylan, sorry about that. I thought you were someone else."

"Katy," he says and I turn around.

He seems as if he literally jumped out of bed and threw on the first T-shirt and jeans he could find and ran here trying to track me down. And I'm sure by the confused and hurt look in his eyes, he is wondering why I left to begin with. I'm not even sure why.

Mimi is between us, holding the door open. She points to him and then me and then back to him and then me one more time.

"Did what I think happened actually happen between you guys last night?" When neither of us answers her, she adds, "Somebody better start talking here."

"Mimi, do you mind?" I ask as nicely as possible given the situation I just walked in on.

She must realize that I'm not in the mood, so she puts her hands in the air in defeat. Before disappearing into her bedroom, she bends down to pick up the paper towels now soaked in coffee from the ground and tosses them in the garbage can.

Then it's just the two of us.

I notice that he still hasn't stepped inside.

"Do you want to come inside?"

"No," he answers quickly.

This throws me off. Because if anything, I think we can maybe talk this through and figure out where we go from here.

"Listen, Dylan," I start, and his demeanor instantly changes. "It's not what you think, I just need some time to think and figure things out. If you just come in and we talk, it—"

"Talk? Talk about what?" In frustration, he runs a hand through his hair and takes a quick breath. He smiles sarcastically and goes on. "Should we talk about how you came over my house last night and we made love for hours? How about we talk about you leaving me this morning as if I were a one-night stand? Or maybe we can talk about how you're always playing with my fucking head and I've had it with this shit? How about we talk about all of *that* before we talk about any other excuses you want to throw my way."

"It's not like that, Dylan. I swear, it's not."

"Then what is it like?"

I struggle to find the right words to make all of this go back to the way it was. But I can't. The look in his eyes tells me that no matter what I say, it won't be enough and won't make sense to him. Hell, how can I explain when it doesn't even make sense to me?

"You know what, Katy? Don't bother." He starts to walk away from me, stopping only once to say, "Just leave me the hell alone."

And then he turns around and leaves for good.

The worst part is that I don't even stop him. I can't because he's right, I royally screwed things up. My friendship with Dylan, which has always meant the world to me, is ruined.

This is bad enough in and of itself. But what hurts more is the knowledge that I threw the wrecking ball.

CHAPTER TWENTY-FOUR

"Leave me alone," I shout, huddled underneath my blanket.

I've been hiding in my bedroom since yesterday morning, only coming out to use the bathroom. Every ounce of energy is gone. Every piece of me hurts, literally. Which I have to laugh at, because I've read books where they say stuff like "my heart hurts," and I'd thought: How in the hell can your heart hurt unless you're having an actual heart attack? It's impossible.

Or at least I thought it was impossible. Because the pain that I feel in my chest is real. It's as real as anything I've ever felt before. And I'm the one who created it.

Why am I so stupid? Why didn't I go about this in a more civilized manner rather than rushing over to Dylan's and skipping right to the good stuff? Sex and friendship are not something you should ever mix . . . and I knew this. But I couldn't help myself.

I felt something.

More than lust and more than friendship, but is it really love?

It's ironic how the tables have turned and now I'm Conner from nine years ago and Dylan is me, unsure and angry at how things have played out. He doesn't deserve any of this. And I wish more than anything that I could talk to him, but the disgusted look on his face when he left here yesterday pretty much told me that ship had sailed. I can't blame him. I'm disgusted with myself too.

Not to mention that I haven't even begun to tackle the whole Conner situation and how I left things between us. I can't imagine what he must be thinking of me . . . or I should say, how little he thinks of me right now.

A soft tap at my door startles me. Mimi tried getting me to open the door yesterday, but I refused. So she should know better than to try it again today.

"I said, leave me alone!"

"Open the door, Katy," Jonathan says.

At the sound of his voice, I start to tear up. Because if there is anyone I can't refuse, it's him. And knowing that I'm going to have to tell him everything makes me hurt all over again.

When I open the door, Jonathan takes one look at me and sees that it's really, really bad. The tears start to fall when he opens it farther and takes a step inside. As he closes it behind him, I walk backward until the backs of my knees hit my footboard and I plop down. My hands automatically cover my face as I cry, and I feel him sit beside me. Gently, he wraps his arm around my shoulder and pulls me into his chest, where I cry even harder. The whole time he's rubbing my back and not saying a single word, knowing that I just need to get past this part first before I can start talking.

Once I calm down enough that I can actually talk clearly, I ask, "Did Mimi call you?"

From outside my door in the hallway, she answers, "Yes, I did!"

He chuckles lightly, pulling me away from him slowly to look me over. Then he's ducking his hand into his jeans front pocket for a handkerchief, reaching up to wipe away the tears that are still running down my face.

"I give up," he says with a small smile and hands it to me. "Just keep it."

I use it to wipe my face a little, then hold it in my hands, turning it over and over until I see the cursive monogram on the corner: ML.

"This was dad's?" I ask.

"Yeah, I found them when we packed up all of their stuff years ago. I have a couple more at home."

I bring it up to my nose, and even with the stuffiness from crying, I can still catch the faintest trace of Old Spice, my dad's signature scent.

"Thank you," I say as the tears start up again.

"I didn't mean to make you cry more than you already were, Katy. Sorry."

I gather myself once more and wave him off. "Don't be sorry, it's no use at this point, as you can see."

"So."

He lets the word hang. Then, without further prodding from Jonathan, I tell him everything. And I mean everything. So to say that I am mildly embarrassed about crossing the final frontier of talking about sex with my brother would be an understatement. But to his credit, he just sits and listens. He doesn't interrupt me and doesn't say a single word until I'm done.

"Wow."

"You can say that again."

Then he turns to me with a look of disbelief. "All of this happened after I left the game the other night?"

I nod.

"I don't know if I should be impressed or horrified."

"If it helps, I'm horrified," I say.

"What are you going to do?"

"I don't know."

"I've said this to you before, and I'll say this to you again . . . that's a child's answer. You're a grown woman. You can't bank on 'I don't know' for the rest of your life. The rest of your life is now. You need to figure out what you're going to do and figure it out fast."

"I hate when you lawyer up, because it makes it that much more difficult to counter your argument." I fall back onto my bed in frustration and throw an arm across my eyes. "Jonathan, how can I even go to work tomorrow and face him?"

"I don't know, but you're going to have to hold your chin up and do it." He hesitates to say the rest. "I warned you about that, Katy. You can't just expect to sleep with your boss and pretend it's not a big deal . . . no matter if he's your friend or not."

"I know."

Then he's quiet for a few beats before he asks about the other player in this. "What about Conner?"

"I'm going to have to see him before he leaves this week, I guess. I just haven't figured out when or how I'm going to do that, as you can tell by the fact that I've been in the same clothes for almost three days."

"How do you think that will go over?" he asks.

With a sigh, I uncover my eyes and sit back up. "Honestly, I don't know."

"Do you love Conner?"

Do I?

I think the answer was pretty obvious the other night when Dylan's face was dancing around my head as Conner kissed me. If that's not proof that at least I'm not in love or crushing on him, I don't know what is. That doesn't take away the fact that I let him kiss me and I kissed him back the same night that I slept with my best friend, Dylan.

"No, I'm not in love with Conner. I'm sure of it."

"But you feel something for him," he says more than asks.

"I think so . . . not love, definitely not that," I explain, shaking my head. "But there's something special in our past, something that warrants enough of my attention and yes, feelings, that I can't let him leave without talking to him about it."

"Okay, fair enough. Now, let's talk about Dylan."

"Yeah, let's," comes a muffled response from the other side of the door, which I don't even bother to acknowledge.

"I think I'm in love with him."

"You think or you are? There's a big difference."

"I know there's a big difference, I'm not stupid." He raises an eyebrow. "Okay, okay, I may be acting stupid about it and going about it all wrong, but here's the thing. I think I'm in love with him and have been in love with him for some time, but it's hard to separate whether or not I was motivated because I was afraid of losing him as a friend or being replaced by another woman, in this case Rachel. It's like seeing something for the very first time without rose-tinted glasses on, and you're like, 'Whoa, where have you been all my life?' But he's been there all along, and that's what makes changing the nature of our relationship from one day to the next so difficult for me to figure out." I take a big gulp of air and grip the handkerchief in my hand a little tighter. "I think that's why I freaked out and left him yesterday. I just needed a minute to make sure that I was doing the right thing, because the thought of not having him in my life is something I don't think I can bear. Actually, I know it's something I can't bear."

"You do realize that sleeping with him was probably not the best decision you ever made, right?" he asks. "And trust me, yes, I'm having a very hard time talking to you about this."

This makes me smile a little. "I know I probably should have thought things out before running over to his place the other night. I can't explain it. It's like if I didn't go over there right then and there, I felt like I was going to die. Does that make sense?"

"As crazy as that sounds, yes, it makes perfect sense."

"It does?"

"Yes, because it definitely sounds like you're in love. But you're going to have to fix your relationship and be very careful." He pulls my chin up to look at him. "Mimi said Dylan was devastated and didn't want anything more to do with you when he came by here yesterday morning."

I squint at Mimi through the door like I'm Superman. "Did you tell Jonathan what else happened yesterday? Or did you conveniently forget that part?"

"Are you talking about Mimi with Simon?" Jonathan asks.

My head turns so fast that I almost get dizzy. "You knew? And you never told me?"

The corners of his lips curl up in a sly smile. "Let's just say that I've caught Simon in a lie or two when it comes to his personal life and leave it at that."

"It actually makes perfect sense when I think about it. I kind of like the idea of the two of them together, but don't tell them I said so. I want to be mad at them for a little while longer."

"I heard that and love you too!" Mimi shouts from the hallway.

Ignoring her, he asks, "Are you going to be okay?"

I blow my nose into the handkerchief and take a few gulps of air to clear my head. Then, as much as I hate to admit to it, I actually do feel that it's eventually going to be okay one way or the other. Just getting there is the tricky part.

"Yeah, I think so," I say and reach over to wrap my arms around his neck. "Thank you, Jonathan."

He squeezes me tight and kisses the top of my head, telling me to call him if I need anything else. Then he's gone, and as I watch him leave, I think to myself how much I wish that Jonathan would find the right woman. Because nobody that sweet and caring should be single . . . and that whoever he does end up with better treat him like gold. If not, she's going to have to deal with me.

CHAPTER TWENTY-FIVE

When I arrive at the newsroom on Monday morning a little later than usual, I'm nervous and anxious and terrified. But somehow, I think through the magic of Jonathan's encouraging words and pep talk, I feel good about what I'm planning to do. My intention is to have a real heart-to-heart with Dylan about everything. Everything from finding out how he really feels about me, to realizing that I feel the same way, to acting on all those feelings the other night, to screwing up royally . . . everything. Because I want him. I want us. And I'm willing to face my fears to make it happen.

I'm thankful for the cacophony of the newsroom. My colleagues are talking on the phone and to each other, telephones are buzzing, computers are dinging with incoming and outgoing alerts. As I walk through the maze of desks, the noise keeps me focused on my own desk at the other side of the room instead of trying to sneak a peek into Dylan's office.

I do it anyway.

For a split second before I turn my head, I'm filled with dread at the possibility that Rachel will be at his door with her boobs. As if she would know that she could swoop right in and pick up right where she left off. Which makes me wonder exactly what did happen with them before I got to Dylan's condo the other night and made wild, passionate love to him . . . and then left him like the idiot that I am.

Good going, Katy.

The thought disappears almost as soon as it surfaces in my head, because I spot Dylan across the room, standing at the threshold of his office, staring right back at me. And the look in his eyes is . . . well, it's not good. The tic of his jaw and the frustration in his eyes is evident even from where I stand. Then a slight movement at his side causes my attention to follow and I see his hands clench into fists. He does this a couple of times before turning on his heel and walking back into his office.

The muscles of his back shift underneath the soft cotton of his sky blue dress shirt, and I remember how it felt to have those same muscles bunch underneath my own hands a few nights ago. How it felt to have his body on top of mine, moving slowly and deliberately, as if time stood still for both of us. And finally, how it felt to have him inside of me. Bringing me a pleasure so great that I held on to him tightly, my nails digging into his skin and garnering a low groan from somewhere deep in his throat.

A shiver runs through me as the images flash in my mind.

It shakes me out of my stupor, and I notice that he left the door to his office wide open. This is my chance.

Frozen in the center of the chaos of the newsroom floor and with my emotions going up and down like a roller coaster inside my stomach, I try unsuccessfully to get my legs to start moving toward him. They don't want to cooperate. It's like my body is alerting me to danger ahead and is trying to protect me. However, memories of how he made my body feel provide just the right amount of gumption to propel me forward.

Just a few more steps, I think to myself as my body finally cooperates. It's only nine or ten more steps. My heart jackhammers away in my chest as a bead of sweat trickles down the back of my neck. Three more steps. Two.

And then . . .

"Ms. Lewis." Phoebe's dead-as-the-night-sky voice breaks me out of my ambitious task. "He's busy at the moment."

I ignore her. Not caring if she thinks I'm the biggest bitch in the world right now. My need to get to Dylan is way more important than whatever lowly opinion she may have of me now and forever.

When I walk into his office, I quickly close the door and flip the lock for good measure. Resting my head against the unforgiving hard surface, I hear Dylan curse in frustration under his breath. Closing my eyes, I steel myself for a beat and gather my courage before turning around to face him.

He's sitting behind his desk and looks as if he can't even bear the sight of me. His bright eyes darken behind the black rims of his eyeglasses and speak to me without words. They say that he loves me, always has, but he doesn't want to. They say that he's struggling to keep himself in check. And they tell me that he wants to pretend that nothing happened between us the other night.

The closer I get to him, the more I falter under the weight of everything that has transpired in the past couple of weeks—and maybe even from the very beginning of our relationship. When I reach his desk, I adjust the strap of my messenger bag nervously before meeting his eyes again.

"What do you want, Katy?"

A thrill runs through me at his question. The same one he asked the night I appeared at his doorstep when I wanted nothing more than to be consumed by him.

"I wanted . . . I needed to talk to you about what happened on Friday . . . and Saturday morning. About everything."

I might as well have thrown a lit match on a can of gasoline, because Dylan erupts from his chair, startling me. He stands there for a second before ducking his head down and resting his fists on his desk. A long sigh escapes him when he looks at me again and then runs a hand through his hair in frustration.

"I can't do this anymore," he says with a ring of finality that terrifies me.

"What do you mean you can't do this anymore?" I sound like a stupid little girl even to my own ears. Of course he doesn't want to do *this* anymore. But I need to try to change his mind. "Dylan, I'm sorry."

He barely chuckles. "You're sorry?"

"Yes, I needed to tell you that. And I need to tell you—"

"Don't you understand that whatever you think you 'need' to tell me doesn't matter? You blew it, Katy. All this time, you've *been* blowing it. You never picked up your head long enough to see that I've been here waiting for you . . . wanting you." He pauses, then grabs on to the edge of his desk with such force that for a moment I think he might break it in half. "Do you have any idea what it's like to be in love with your best friend and not once have that person realize that you feel that way? Do you have any clue or the slightest inkling as to what it felt like to have you in my bed finally after all these years? Then wake up to find you gone? And for what? To fucking think?"

In a small voice, I say to him, "I didn't know you felt that way, Dylan. Why didn't you tell me?"

"Really? Then why did you pull that little stunt last week?"

His eyebrow arches in challenge.

"Rachel." I say her name out loud the moment she pops into my thoughts. "Because I didn't want you to be with her and I needed to stop her from trying. And you from noticing her."

"Are you serious?" He laughs out loud. Then Dylan comes around the desk slowly, stalking toward me while I almost wither under the pressure of his intense stare. When he's right in front of me, I lower my head again. His hand comes up and softly takes hold of my chin, which he lifts to meet his eyes. He quietly says, "How the hell can I notice

Rachel when all I see is you? All I've *ever* seen is you from the moment you walked through my door and into my life."

Tears well up in my eyes. I feel like a complete bitch for being so relieved that he doesn't want Rachel in that way. Because it only validates what Dylan's really trying to say. That I'm selfish and completely blind when it comes to him . . . to us.

"I wish you would have told me. I wish—"

"You wish what, Katy?" He drops his hand from my face. He starts to back away and I immediately miss his touch. "You know what? I don't care what you wish, it's done. Please just get out of my office."

"But I . . . please let me explain. Please give me a chance. It's only fair."

He's already settling back into his chair and ignoring me by focusing his attention on the computer monitor. Then in the most dismissive voice I've ever heard come from Dylan, he says without looking at me, "And the next time you come barging in here, there will be consequences, Ms. Lewis."

Hearing him say my name so formally tears right through me. Watching him type away at his desk as if I I'm not even here, waiting for me to leave his sight, leave his office, leave his life . . . it's too much to bear. The tears I was holding in break free and stream down my face. And that's my cue to leave.

I rub my hands across my cheeks to wipe away the tears and catch his attention one last time before walking to his office door. As I unlock the handle and open the door, he says to my back, "For the record, I did tell you once . . . you just don't remember."

Racking my brain, I mindlessly walk past Phoebe, past my colleagues, past the receptionist, and into the elevator. Once I'm safely inside, the memory finally comes back to me . . .

Two years ago . . .

"Truth or dare?" *Mimi asked with a wiggle of her eyebrows. After filling a drink order at the far end of the bar, she came running back to Dylan and me with such pep in her step that I thought she might trip on the way back.*

Dylan had agreed to meet us that night after closing up shop at the office later than usual. He'd had a really rough week and badly needed to decompress. The moment I asked him out, a smile so wide and bright spread across his face that I couldn't stop from laughing. It was if I had given him the keys to the kingdom. He asked me if I was planning on drinking since he was well aware of the fact that I rarely do. I told him that I had no problem being his designated driver and that he was free to let loose. With that, an even bigger smile appeared.

"Katy," *he'd said earlier that day in his office,* "you are the best."

So there we all were, chatting and trying not to gossip too much about the office and who was dating who and who was supposedly sleeping with this one and that one. When all of a sudden, Mimi wanted to play truth or dare.

Just as she brought it up, another customer called her over. When she left, Dylan asked, "Is she serious? I haven't played that game since I was in tenth grade."

I leaned forward, resting my chin in my hand and enjoying the fact that Dylan was obviously a little tipsy and probably two drinks away from being officially drunk. Make that one drink.

I hadn't seen him that drunk in all the time I'd known him. Not that I condoned being drunk. But it was nice to see him relaxed and not as proper and businesslike as he usually was. As the night—and the drinking—progressed, he loosened his tie and unbuttoned his collar. His sleeves were rolled up and he tried to keep a shot (or two) from spilling on his shirt. But I could see the cherry red stain splashed across his upper chest from the "special shot" that Mimi had made him.

"And how did you do when you played it back then?" I teased.

He closed his eyes and furrowed his brow. Then his eyelids popped open and he said with a mischievous smile, "Second, maybe almost third base with Marianne Carter in her parents' garage."

We both laughed. "And whatever happened to Ms. Marianne Carter? Did you break her heart?"

"Nah, she broke mine," he said. "She left me in the garage and went on to date someone who was older and wiser."

"Like college older?"

"No, more like eleventh grade."

I couldn't stop laughing. And then he was laughing. And then before I knew it, I had that crazy choking kind of laugh that sounded like a snorting pig. This made Dylan laugh even harder.

Until Mimi came back with a serious look on her face and put us on the spot with her question: Truth or dare?

I told her that a truth should be told no matter what. I mean, if you were true friends with a person, why would you be lying to begin with? And a dare? Well, I just don't live dangerously to begin with, so what would be the point?

She squared her shoulders, and with her usual no-nonsense delivery, she said, "Stop being such a downer. Just play the game. It's easy. Watch." She turned to Dylan and asked, "Truth or dare?"

He didn't even hesitate. "Truth."

"Hmmm, let me think. Oh! Okay, I got one!" Mimi gave me a quick wink before asking, "When was the last time you had sex?"

"Oh my God! Mimi!" I was horrified that she chose to open with this question. "Are you kidding me?!" I was about to tell Dylan not to answer, but he was grinning from ear to ear.

"You're a pervert, you know that?" he said to Mimi.

"Yup and proud of it. So tell me the truth, big guy." She rested her elbows on the bar and added, "If you do, I'll give you another shot of my special truth serum."

"Do not answer her," I said at the same time he answered.

"Two, wait, no . . . three weeks ago."

For some reason, Dylan's answer threw me for a loop. I swiveled my head to him, trying to remember if he'd mentioned dating anyone around that time. And I came up blank.

"How was it?" Mimi asked.

I covered my face with my hands. "Please. Stop. Don't."

"What's the big deal, Katy?" she said. "We're all adults here. We adult all day and all night and some of us like to adult in between the sheets . . . against walls and kitchen counters. Bathroom floors at the mall. Gas stations and movie theaters. And—"

"I want to die right now. I really just want the ground to swallow me whole and die. Please just stop it already, it's embarrassing."

"Wait a second," Dylan said, trying not to laugh. "I need to hear the bathroom floor at the mall story."

"Do not encourage her," I said, glaring at Mimi with the evil eye.

She glared right back, then turned her attention to Dylan. "Not so fast, hot stuff. You need to answer my question."

I was curious, but then again, I wasn't sure I wanted to know about that part of Dylan's life. Especially when he could say something he'd regret . . . if he even remembered.

I stood up then and tugged at his sleeve. It took several seconds to break his stare with Mimi, who had a knowing grin on her face. Rolling my eyes at the two of them, I said, "Come on. It's time to go home, Dylan."

"She's such a party pooper, isn't she?" she asked. Then she asked him, "How about one more shot for the road?"

He nodded enthusiastically. I sighed loudly and let them get it over with so I could drive Dylan home and go to bed. Mimi did her usual bartender *party tricks behind the bar, and then, voilà, there was a shot sitting right in front of Dylan.*

He had the decency in his near drunkenness to look up at me as if asking permission to prolong our time at the bar. To which I said, "Go ahead, but be warned that you're the one who's going to suffer the consequences come tomorrow morning."

Dylan ignored my warning and took the shot in hand. Bringing it to his lips, he tipped it back and downed it in a half a second. His throat bobbed up and down when he swallowed, and then he licked his lips as if it had quenched whatever existential thirst he had at that moment.

"Okay, time's up. Let's go." I tugged at his sleeve again. "Good night, Mimi."

It took a bit of work, but I managed to get Dylan into my car without too much of a headache. And before I slid into the driver's seat, he was already asleep.

I had to laugh. He looked so peaceful and cute all curled up into the window. The only thing that snapped me out of my amusement was the very real idea that he might get sick in my car. I immediately stopped laughing and started driving.

When we arrived at his condo, I gently prodded him awake. But he wouldn't budge.

It was one thing to get him from the bar to my car, but it was quite another to get his dead weight out of my car and up to his front door safely. I couldn't do it without him being awake and semi-cooperative. As cute as he looked, being asleep wouldn't work.

Leaning across the console, I tried to whisper loudly in his ear, "Dylan, wake up."

He didn't even bat an eyelash.

I bit my lip, trying to keep my laughter and slight frustration at bay. Leaning in closer, I called his name again a little louder.

This time, his hand twitched in his lap. I figured he was starting to come to, but instead, he reached up and looped his hand around my neck to pull me even closer to him. Like I was his life-sized teddy bear or something.

I started to laugh at his reaction. The fact that Dylan Sterling, editor in chief of the Florida Observer, *liked to cuddle, cracked me up. This revelation would provide me with tons of ammunition if ever I needed it in the future.*

But then I heard him mumble something under his breath. I couldn't make it out over my laughing, so I managed to tear myself out of his grasp and asked him to repeat himself.

"Shhhh wasn't . . ." he mumbled. Then he added yet more to his undecipherable babble. ". . . you."

It was impossible to translate his words since his speech was more like slurring at that point. However, it seemed like hearing himself say whatever he was trying to say was enough to wake him up.

He looked over at me. "Where are we?"

"Your condo. Can you walk to your door or should I call my brother Simon to assist us?"

That seemed to sober him a bit. "Nope, I'm good. Thanks for driving."

"What are friends for?"

Dylan's face turned serious as he reached for the door handle. When he opened it and placed one foot outside, he answered me.

"Everything."

Later that night I realized what he was saying in his sleep. And to this day, I don't know why I thought nothing of what he said in what was obviously a moment of stripped down honesty.

Maybe I didn't want things to change between us. Maybe I wasn't ready. Maybe I thought he was talking about somebody else.

But now, knowing what he said, knowing he meant it and that he had in fact revealed his true feelings for me, I wanted to curl up and die for being so dense.

And today, as the elevator arrives at the first floor of the office building, I say the same three words out loud to myself that Dylan told me two years ago . . .

"She wasn't you."

CHAPTER TWENTY-SIX

I work from home for the next couple of days, opting to take full advantage of current technology rather than having to face Dylan.

I'm being a chickenshit like Mimi has repeatedly reminded me, but it's the only way to not lose my job while I try to work things out.

The slight cringing I experience comes late Wednesday afternoon when I press Send on an e-mail to Dylan with a finished article. It takes a few minutes of staring at my inbox, waiting for Dylan's comments, to get a response:

Thanks and feel better.

"Well, at least he's hoping I'm not dying or anything," I say out loud to myself.

Then I instantly feel awful because I'm reminded that Dylan has stopped sending me his daily texts. I expected it, but it still hurts deeply to know that every little thing that made us *us* is gone. I want a do-over. I need to go back and tell him that I do love him and that I do want to be with him. I want these things more than anything. But I don't know how to do it. Frustrated with myself beyond belief, I decide to tackle one problem at a time.

Conner . . .

Okay, I can put this baby to rest once and for all.

I text him, asking to meet up at our old stomping ground. I'm hoping that he responds, given the fact that I've been ignoring his calls and texts since Friday night. If he doesn't answer, well, at least I have the peace of mind that I tried to make amends before he goes home to California.

His text comes almost too fast, catching me a bit off guard:

I'll see you at the playground in twenty minutes, Shadow.

I arrive at the park at dusk to find Conner already waiting for me. He sits on a swing, his legs way too long to fit comfortably and crossed at the ankles. He sees me coming and smiles, then motions to his left at the empty swing next to him.

"I saved you a seat," he says.

"Thanks."

Sitting down, my legs dangle long enough to anchor me to the ground so I don't swing too much. I glance over at Conner, who's watching my every move and waiting for me to say something.

"So are you ready to go back home?"

"Yes and no," he says. "I'm ready to get back to work, but I'm not ready to leave you again."

Well, I guess we're getting right to it then.

"Conner, I—"

"No, listen to me for once, okay?" he asks. "I need to explain."

"Okay."

"Shadow, sorry, I mean Katy."

"Conner, you don't have to stop calling me Shadow. I've missed it."

Smiling now, he nods at my request. "Okay, so I've been thinking about it. About us, about when we were kids and how everything kind of changed and the letter and—"

"I still have it, you know."

I don't know why I tell him this, but I feel like it's important that he knows how much it meant to me all these years. Even if the outcome wasn't something I wanted, I can look back on my time with Conner and smile, because he meant so much to me and still does.

"When I heard your voice mail that first day you called me out of the blue, I read it again for the first time in years." I laugh in embarrassment. "I still can't believe I did that."

"It was the best letter anyone has ever written me, Shadow."

I stop laughing just as quickly as I had started.

"I only wish I had done something about it sooner," he says. There's a long stretch of comfortable silence between us. "The other night at my house, I'm sorry if I spooked you."

"I wouldn't say that *you* spooked me, Conner. I think I spooked myself."

"How do you mean?"

I look up to the now night sky and kick my legs out from underneath me. I swing once, twice, and then stop, anchoring my feet in the soft dirt to keep me from moving again. "Because I'm not that girl anymore. That girl had wished and hoped for you to say those things to her at some point . . . but that time has passed. I moved on and so did you. And all of that is okay, because if anything, this short time again with you has reminded me how much I missed you as a friend."

"Do you think we could stay friends this time around?" he asks. "I'm being serious. I don't want to lose you again, Shadow."

"Well, that depends," I say.

"Depends on what?"

"Depends on if *you* actually keep in touch. See, they have this thing nowadays called e-mail. It's really new and exciting and makes it easy to stay in contact with people you care about."

He laughs before his expression turns serious again. "I meant what I said, though. I screwed up with you in the past, and I don't intend to let it happen again. I want to know everything that's going on with you . . . maybe not everything. But you know what I mean, right?"

"Like old times."

"Just like old times, Katy."

We sit on the swings not saying another word to each other for a moment, then Conner spins in his swing so he can look behind us. Then he spins right back to face me, and the spark that lights up his hazel eyes reminds me of how he looked on that very first day we met.

"So, I was just going to go across the street and get a Gatorade or something." He stands up.

He offers me his hand, and when I put mine in his, it's next to impossible to hide the smile on my face.

"Shouldn't we tell my brothers we're leaving?" I ask, laughing. "I don't know if I should trust you."

"You can trust me, Shadow . . . you can always trust me."

CHAPTER TWENTY-SEVEN

I t's been a few days since I've seen or spoken to my best friend, Dylan. The man I'm in love with.

Who also happens to be my boss.

And who also probably hates my guts.

As confusing and as daunting as all of that is, I still manage to get all my work done. And this week, since the Barracudas play on Thursday night instead of their usual Friday night, I'm able to make the game and finish my article in more than enough time to make Friday's morning edition.

Which leaves me with a day open to do nothing but think.

And think some more about Dylan, of course.

I worry how our boss/employee relationship will affect my career. Being taken seriously in an overwhelmingly male populated environment hasn't been easy. And if word gets out that I slept with my editor in chief, my professional reputation will suffer the most. And all the respect I've gained from my colleagues from the hard work and late nights I've put in to dispel their ideas that I'm his favorite or that I'm not good enough goes flying out the window. So on the off chance that I finally get an opportunity to speak to him, I'm hoping that we can agree to keep the work side of our relationship on track.

On a better note, at least one part of my life has gotten squared away and resolved. Conner and I said our good-byes and exchanged contact information. Until he came back into my life, I never realized how much I actually needed to talk to him about that night and give us the closure we both needed. But more than that, the void in my life where my oldest best friend had been is filled again. I want to be able to confide in him like when were growing up, and I believe him when he says he'll keep in touch. And if he doesn't keep up his end of the bargain, I told him I would fly out to LA and kick his ass again in tag football and embarrass him in front of all of his friends.

Then my mind goes back to Dylan. The fact that he hasn't reached out to me has not gone unnoticed. I've been thinking a lot about the day we met and how every day since then has been filled with him in some capacity. And as much as I miss him as a friend, I know with a hundred percent certainty that I want more than that. I want him not only as my friend but my lover and to be there when I wake up in the morning and go to bed at night.

I want all of these things and then some.

I want Dylan. I love him.

But I'm too scared to tell him to his face.

That's why I'm sitting here alone on the couch and mindlessly flipping the channels on the television after sending off my article to him.

When Mimi strolls in a little later than usual, because she was obviously with Simon—the cat coming out of the bag on that one in a way I'll never forget—I'm surprised but glad to see her, since I could use the company.

"What'cha doing?" She sits next to me.

"Nothing."

"What'cha watching?"

"Nothing."

Then a few minutes pass before she rips the remote out of my hand and turns off the television.

"Hey, I was watching that!"

"Really? What were you watching?" she asks, raising an eyebrow defiantly.

I rack my brain, trying to pinpoint one of the hundreds of stations I was browsing through and can't think of anything. So I say, "Something."

"Real mature, Katy. Real mature." She chucks the remote on the other side of her, then looks at me with those caramel eyes narrowed, as if she is trying to put me in a trance. "Look, it's really easy. Just get off of your ass and go to him already. I'm sick of seeing you mope around here and feeling sorry for yourself. And I'm sick of seeing Dylan moping around too, for that matter. The both of you are ridiculous, do you know that?"

"You've seen him?" I ask, startled. "How did he look? What did he say?"

"Girl, you don't want to know."

I look at her with a death stare. "If I didn't want to know, I wouldn't have asked. Come on, tell me, please?"

"It's your funeral." She sighs dramatically and then says, "Well, he looked like shit and not at all like himself. He hasn't shaved in a couple of days and has some serious stubble going on, and now that I think about it, it kind of makes him a little dangerous looking and a lot hot . . . hotter than usual and—"

"Stop! Just skip to the part where he spoke to you about it instead."

"Fine, relax, I was just getting to that part. He basically said that you tore out his heart and spit on it and then burned it into tiny ashes that are now scattered all over the ends of the earth."

I stare at her incredulously. "He did not say all of that. Did he?"

"He might as well have." She stops and turns in her seat to face me. "Katy, you broke his heart, how do you expect him to feel?"

"I know I did, but . . . but I'm hurt too."

I feel like the asshole that Mimi thinks I am right now. I can tell that she wants to call me some name or another by the look of disbelief in her eyes. But she bites her tongue and realizes she doesn't need to say a word since I'm already feeling like the biggest heel in history and the worst best friend to boot.

"I'm sorry, I shouldn't have said that." I falter for a second, then say, "I want to fix this with him, more than anything. But it's not that easy, Mimi. He won't talk to me."

She laughs.

"What is so funny about that? It's true." I lean across her to where my messenger bag is resting against the sofa on the floor. Pulling out my iPad, I swipe and touch keys until I reach my e-mail and put it in front of her face. "See! I've sent him e-mails and nothing. He doesn't answer me. It's pointless."

"Katy, Katy, Katy, you have the power right there in your hands to make things happen, and yet you sit here and pretend that you don't know what to do."

"What does that mean?" I ask.

She points to the iPad. "You're a writer, figure it out."

Then she gets up and goes to her bedroom, leaving me on the couch to figure out what the hell she means. I look at the iPad again and then over my shoulder to where she disappeared . . . I do this a few times until an idea registers in my head.

I *am* a writer. And if he won't answer my e-mail, he'll answer my letter . . . he'll have no choice.

Checking the time, I have just enough of it left to make the deadline for the Sunday morning edition. But first, I have to make a call and hope that I can get someone to do me the hugest favor in the world.

Florida Observer: Letters to the Editor, Sunday, September 27, 2015

Dear Mr. Sterling,

It is with a heavy heart that I put pen to paper and write this letter to you.

Here it goes . . . I'm in love with my boss who happens to be my best friend.

But I don't know what to do because I think I've screwed things up between us.

How can I tell him that I want to be with him every waking moment of the day and then fall asleep in his arms? How can I tell him that if he asks me again not to go in the middle of the night, that I never will? How can I tell him that I want more than friendship?

Tell me, please, because I can't lose him.

Always,
Your Katy

P.S. Turn around.

CHAPTER TWENTY-EIGHT

I sit nervously inside of my car, watching Dylan as he gets ready to read the Sunday newspaper.

I know his schedule like the back of my hand. And if there is one thing, without fail, that he does like clockwork, it's come Sunday morning, he'll buy the newspaper and come to the beach to sit and read it from start to finish.

So when Mimi called me out, I knew that I had one shot to get the letter printed in the Sunday edition. Luckily, I'm friendly with the person in the office who controls the printings. After a last-minute call to him on Friday night and an endless amount of promises that I would never ever be late on a deadline again, he agreed to run my letter in the "Letters to the Editor" section without Dylan's final approval.

Of course he was terrified of the repercussions and made me swear up and down that if the higher-ups or Dylan himself had a problem with any of it, I would take the fall. And at that point, once the letter was printed and out there, there would be no question of the way I feel about Dylan, my boss. So the repercussions for me would be tenfold no matter the outcome. But I decided that he, *us*, is worth the risk. And I completely realize that the prospect that I may very well be without a job soon is something I should be worried about a lot more than I am. However, the fear of losing the man I love for good is decidedly worse. I can always work elsewhere, or do something else in the field that will keep me going until another job materializes. But I couldn't just sit there and let him slip through my fingers. So I chose to shout my feelings for him from the rooftops. Go big or go home.

I woke up at the crack of dawn and practically ran out the door to beat Dylan to the beach and get a spot where I could hide.

And like clockwork, Dylan showed up.

It's the first time I've seen him since I left his office on Monday morning. And the sight of him makes my pulse race and my heart thump away in my chest as if it had been asleep for the past week. The urge to run over to him is overwhelming. It starts as this tiny fire in my belly, then spreads to my limbs. Then it builds and builds until it's all consuming and my legs itch to start sprinting. But I can't. Not yet. Not until he actually wants me to. Because this plan can easily backfire, and not just for us but for my career too.

I wait and wait, watching as he turns over page after page, folding them over perfectly with deft hands so that the winds won't keep him from reading. From time to time, he stops and looks out over the water. I can't tell what he's thinking, but I'm hoping somewhere in his mind and his heart there is still room for me . . . for us.

Then, an hour into sitting and pretty much stalking him, he turns around, looking to his left and his right. Which is my cue.

Gathering all the strength I can, I say a little prayer under my breath, close my eyes, and open my car door. Before I second-guess myself, I start walking. He spots me easily and stands up, brushing the sand off his shorts and then adjusting his glasses.

Once I reach the edge of where the pavement meets the sand, I take off my flip-flops and hold them in my hand so I can walk the rest of the way to him. It's a cloudy day and the wind starts to pick up the closer I get to him and the shore. With my heart in my throat, I finally reach him.

And when I look at him today, now, forever . . . I know that he's the man of my dreams, my best friend and my soul mate. His eyes look back at me with vague curiosity, like he can't believe I'm really here standing right in front of him. The smallest hint of relief washes across his features before going right back to the expressionless look that I've come to know all too well over the years.

"I read your letter."

My small smile is to hide the sinking feeling I get after hearing the way he says this: as if it doesn't matter how or what I write to him, he'll never forgive me.

"Oh, okay, so I'll just leave you alone then."

I turn around quickly and start walking back to my car, as if the sand was actually as hot as it usually is on a warm summer's day. Behind me, I hear Dylan's footsteps, so I stop but I can't make myself turn around to face him again. I know that if I do, I'll cry, because my heart feels as if it were literally breaking in two.

I can feel the warmth rolling off of him in waves as he comes even closer, and closer still. And then he's turning me around as my tears well up in anticipation of him saying all of the things I don't want to hear out loud: that he wants nothing more to do with me, that I've ruined any chance we had once and for all.

Dylan's hand surprises me and cups the side of my face. His eyes follow the lone tear that leaks free and down my cheek. When his thumb reaches out to catch it before it hits the ground, I almost break down in relief. Because his green eyes are alive with something more than friendship, something more than a promise, and something more than the right here and now.

"Katy, I think this is the beginning of a beautiful friendship."

And before he can even finish repeating one of the very first things he's ever said to me, I'm in his arms where I belong, always.

EPILOGUE

One Year Later

Florida Observer: Letters from the Editor, Sunday, October 11, 2016

> *Dear Your Katy,*
>
> *Sorry it has taken me so long to write you back.*
>
> *I only have one question, and if you get it right, I'll agree to marry you.*
>
> *In 1977, Miami quarterback Bob Griese was the first NFL player to wear what in a game?*
>
> *Sincerely,*
> *Editor in Chief Dylan Sterling*
>
> *P.S. I made it easy on purpose. Now, turn around.*

ACKNOWLEDGMENTS

Thank you to my kids, my husband, and my friends who have stuck by me and kept me going. A special thanks to the following people, without whom I would lose my mind: Lisa Chamberlin, MJ Abraham, Claire Contreras, Stephanie Sandra Brown, and Sara Queen.

A heartfelt thanks to Melody Guy . . . you are simply amazing and I hope to work with you again one day.

Thanks to everyone at Montlake Romance, specifically my editor, Christopher Werner, who I've probably driven crazy with titles for this book, and by the time it goes to print, covers too. Jessica Poore, author relations representative, who is without a doubt one of the most thoughtful and funny people I've had the pleasure of never meeting in person. And finally, my original editor, Maria Gomez, thank you for believing in me and rooting for me from the sidelines.

Thanks to my readers, who somehow get my sick sense of humor and send me notes to let me know how much they laughed and cried during one of my books. Those notes never get old, and no matter how much time goes by, I'm still humbled that you chose my book out of the thousands you could be reading instead.

And finally, thanks to all the book bloggers out there, big or small, who support me and my books. Without you, I would be nowhere, and to say that I appreciate each and every one of you would be an understatement. I would, however, like to say a special thanks to a specific few who have come to mean a lot more to me than I could possibly put into words: Sandy Roman Borrero, Holly Malgieri, Kayla Sunday, Cantu Sisters (Amanda and Crystal), Stephanie Brown, and AJ too! (Hi, AJ!!) Christine Estevez, and finally, Angie McKeon.